Magnificent Desolation

Also by John Robinson

Love Letters Unsent to People Unmet, a book of poetry

Mystics on the Road to Vanishing Point, a novel

Dark Blue Monstropolis, online fiction project

Love Letters and *Mystics* are both available
in unabridged audiobook form as well.
See http://www.onetusk.com for more details.

Dark Blue Monstropolis can be found at
http://www.darkbluemonstropolis.com.

Magnificent Desolation

short stories
by John Robinson

ONE TUSK PUBLISHING
Atlanta, Georgia

This book is a work of fiction. All the names, characters, places and events portrayed in this book are fictitious. Any resemblance to actual events or locales, or people, living or dead, is purely coincidental.

"Adelaide" originally appeared in Altered Perceptions, 1999.
"Necrogarchy" originally appeared on CHUD.com, 2000.
"Voodoo ver. 1.0" originally appeared in Alphadrive 002, 1998.

MAGNIFICENT DESOLATION

Copyright 1996–2004 by John Robinson.
All rights reserved. No part of this book may be reproduced in any form or by any means, except for the inclusion of brief quotations in a review, without permission in writing from the publisher.

Cover Art by Studio Three.
Photo logistics assistance by Ron and Ann Leith.
Photo shoot security by John and Nancy Robinson.

Published by One Tusk Productions
2900 Delk Rd., Ste. 700#289
Marietta, Georgia 30067
USA

ISBN # 0-9747440-6-9

Printed in the United States of America.

For Jenna.

Contents

Necrogarchy	1
Kora	20
The Last Burden	33
The Day They Let Bernard Leave	45
Adelaide	56
Voodoo ver. 1.0	62
Of Sorcery and Seasoning	73
Bottom's	86
Things No One Should Know	96
These Modern Times	105
Room 814	112
Grey	123
The Excavation	135
With Such Permanence As Time Has	146

Necrogarchy

Thompson's eyes snapped open and he stood up quickly, his head ringing with the sudden shift from lightly dozing to fully aware. He looked out through the chain link fence.

No.

There was nothing unusual out there. A couple of figures shambled by, pausing only for a second to glance at him before continuing along their uncomprehending way.

He took a moment to again thank God they no longer stopped and stared like they used to. That was something he had never quite managed to get comfortable with.

Thompson brushed dirt from his pants, then looked up at the overcast sky. It had been nothing but grey clouds for the past week or so, with not a single drop of rain. There was no sign of it clearing up anytime soon, either. He shook his head.

Out of the corner of his eye he saw Jared trotting carefully toward him. Despite the fact the streets outside were calm for the moment, you never wanted to take chances and draw undue attention to yourself. Thompson's father had always told him not to push sticks into ant hills and be surprised when he wound up with red, stinging welts on his ankles.

Jared arrived on the scene, breath escaping from his mouth in small clouds, his eyes wide. "You okay, chief?"

Thompson found being called "chief" amusing enough to let slide and not annoying enough to dissuade. Still, every time Jared called him that, Thompson came close to mentioning that he had an M-16 slung over one shoulder and not a bow, a tomahawk, or even a firehose.

"Yeah, Jay, I'm fine." They spoke in low whispers, as was the custom. Orders were not to speak in regular conversational tones unless within the inner perimeter.

"Well," Jared continued, stealing a look through the fence, "I saw you jump up and thought you might have seen something. So I came over."

So you came over, Thompson repeated in his mind. *Like you ever need an excuse to wander from your post.* Jared was a good kid, but he was just that: a kid. He was only eighteen and had the attention span to prove it. Eighteen was the age the Council wanted you to reach so they could slap a weapon in your hand and call you a man. The weapon in question the Council had seen fit to give Jared was a .45 automatic pistol, kept securely in the young man's shoulder holster. *Thank Christ he finally started remembering to put the safety on,* Thompson thought.

"Didn't see anything," Thompson replied. "To be honest, I thought I might have heard something."

Jared's eyes grew wider, more from eagerness than fear. He had not gotten a chance to use his pistol yet, and Thompson knew he was on the lookout for the opportunity. "Like what?"

Thompson asked himself the question. *Like what?* He was not certain. He had been almost fully asleep, so there was the off-chance he had been dreaming. Considering how many of them were out there beyond the fence, wandering around the abandoned shops and offices, the idea that one of them simply knocked something over was not a far fetched one. He thought back to the day a large one started sliding a desk around the street, not certain of what to do with it, other than shove it from one place to another. Thompson and the others had watched from their posts, each of them certain he would figure out how to use it as a ram against the gate. He had not.

"Jay, I don't know, could've been nothing." Thompson shrugged.

"Maybe so," Jared said, very seriously. "I didn't hear anything."

Uh-huh, Thompson replied inwardly. He was surprised the kid could hear at all. Despite the moratorium placed on wasting batteries, Jared would still find ways to get power to his dilapidated boom box. He slapped on headphones full of Blue Oyster Cult and Van Halen and would play them at ear-shock levels.

He had told Thompson just two weeks before, with breathless anticipation, of how the solar committee might give him the ability to work off of AC power once they got some cells going. Thompson was sure this would give Jared all the excuse he needed to blast what remained of his eardrums to kingdom come.

"So it was nothing," Thompson agreed. "Get back over to your post before someone finds you gone."

Jared nodded. "Aye, aye, chief." With a quick and clumsy salute, he was jogging back to the north face of town.

Thompson shook his head and wanted to laugh but did not. Laughter most assuredly would bring the things outside to see what was happening but regardless, the humor was inappropriate. Jared would have been severely chastised for being away from his post, while Thompson himself apparently could do no wrong.

Two weeks previous, he had fallen asleep on the job as he had today, only to be awoken by none other than the Mayor.

Thompson had jumped, frightened and wide-eyed. One hand had instinctively reached for his sidearm.

"Whoa, whoa, easy." The Mayor took a step backwards with his hands in the air. "Easy there, general." His expression was not one of worry; he was smiling.

"Mayor," Thompson replied, dropping his hand from his pistol. "I'm sorry, I was just—" But that was just it, wasn't it? He wasn't just doing anything but sleeping, so what was he assuming he might put over on the Mayor? Although the Mayor wasn't the Commander, Thompson's direct superior, they were both on the Council. Word of his transgression would no doubt be passed along accordingly. Thompson waited calmly for his reprimand.

The Mayor surprised Thompson by winking at him. "No need to apologize, my boy." He further surprised Thompson by grinning at him, as if they were sharing some illicit secret. "In some cases, falling asleep during one's day job is an acceptable thing—as long as their night job is panning out. Eh?" Thompson at this point half-expected the Mayor to nudge him with an elbow.

Thompson must have turned red, although he could not have sworn to it. "I understand, sir. Thank you."

The Mayor then clapped the young man on the arm before walking away.

The truth was that Thompson did understand. And unfortunately, so did everyone else in the City. The total population of the City was eighty-four. Like any other small town—protected from the outside world by a razor wire-crowned chain link fence and armed guards or not—news got around quickly. Few were unaware that Thompson had been courting the young schoolteacher who had come from St. Louis for sanctuary.

Sally spent her days tutoring the few children there were in the City, and then spent her nights with that nice young Sergeant Thompson. The Council was behind procreation one hundred and ten percent. Their numbers were small enough as it was, so someone had to get on with the business of beefing up the species once more. As a result, even when the Mayor would find Thompson asleep at his post, he would smile and keep on strolling.

Thompson was tired again today, but not for the reasons his fellow citizens might suspect. He and Sally spent most of their night discussing the ramifications of bringing a child into the world of perpetual standoff that the City had become. Thompson had appealed both to the love that they shared and to their civic responsibility, but Sally was not so easily convinced. They had finished their discussion in the moments before dawn, leaving Thompson with no time to rest before going on duty.

He had tried to reassure Sally, and perhaps himself as well, that it was the right thing to do. They had guards on duty constantly to make sure the perimeter was secure. If there was an outburst or emergency, they had two generators hooked up to the outer perimeter that could provide enough juice to cook anything that laid hands upon it. The masses outside had been convinced the City was nothing they wanted a part of. They merely stayed back at a distance of ten feet and shambled about from place to place aimlessly. It had been six months since any gunfire was necessary at the gate.

At least, that's the amount of time that seemed to have passed. The battery to Thompson's own wristwatch had expired long ago, and a couple of people who had bothered to write out their own calendars seemed to differ by a day or so. The Mayor, if you asked him the date, would no doubt tell you it was March the fifteenth, the year 1997. Still, doubt danced behind the certainty he wore on his face.

Sally pointed out it had been longer still since a live visitor had arrived at the gate, seeking sanctuary. She looked out the window to the rest of the world, which they both knew to be completely dark and filled with shambling bodies. He wanted to counter with Fort McMurtrie, with the short-wave link they had with someone outside the City, but he could not. They had not spoken with anyone from McMurtrie for two weeks, and no one talked about it because of what it portended. Radio trouble, they mumbled amongst themselves, but somehow no one believed it.

Thompson looked west into what had been Green Street, but there was nothing to see. Another four hours and his shift would be over. He could go home and take a nap, and when Sally returned—

He looked up sharply. A quick glance to his right showed Jared looking out through the fence, also startled. Jared's eyes met Thompson's and he made a pistol with his hand.

It had been a gunshot.

Before another moment passed, something rounded the corner three blocks down and began bolting toward them at breakneck speed. It took Thompson's mind longer than it should have to recognize it.

It was a horse and rider.

"Son of a bitch," he breathed.

Jared came sprinting from his post. "Chief, are you—"

"—seeing what you're seeing, yes." Thompson hit the alarm bell with one hand and the din from inside the inner perimeter rudely split the stillness.

Jared went for the gate switch but Thompson grabbed his arm. "Not yet," he said evenly. "We wait for the others. I don't want all of that myself." He jerked his head toward the gate, where the shuffling bodies had stopped their wandering and were eyeing the two men warily.

In the distance, the corpses were swarming out of every possible portal to try and bar the rider's passage. The man had the reins in his teeth and was urging the horse onward with his heels. In each hand he held a pistol and was firing with incredible accuracy at the advancing hordes. As Thompson took precious moments watching, one cadaver became a shambling creature only from the neck down.

"Start thinning them," Thompson called to Jared.

Jared looked back at him, paralyzed.

"Move!" Thompson ordered, and the sharpness in his tone finally drew the young man into action.

Jared drew his pistol, clicked back the safety and pushed it through a hole in the chain links. He squinted one eye and fired. A cloud of dust and black spray erupted from the shoulder of a nearby corpse. He tried again and the mottled head attached to the shoulder exploded in a flash of bone and blood, leaving the body to fall like a puppet with severed strings.

Thompson raised his own weapon and began to fire into the bodies closest to the gate, but there were far too many of them to make an effective dent in the oncoming forms. He dropped three of them, neat holes appearing in the skulls of the attackers, the other side of their heads blowing outwards.

A seeming eternity later, three other men and two women joined the melee and Thompson hit the gate switch. The rider was a block away now and gaining speed. He was also dealing with a denser crowd of assailants. At one moment, a corpse managed to grab hold of a stirrup but its wrist snapped away from the rest of its arm.

The gate moved the few feet necessary for the horse and rider to enter. All those at the gap were firing into the crowd of zombies, which were divided between going for the incoming meal or trying for the group behind the relative safety of the fence. The only thing that seemed to slow the attackers' progress was the fact that one would fall and block their path. Still, moments later five others would crawl over the body to take its place. Thompson called out to the oncoming rider, "Come on, get in here!"

The rider came through the opening in the gate at a full run and was bringing his horse to a halt as Thompson hit the switch for the gate to close once more. The attackers were not letting up and kept trying to force themselves through the breach, despite the constant gunfire.

The gate slid back into place and Thompson yelled over the din. "Get clear! Get clear!" The defenders backed away from the fence quickly, freeing Thompson to press another button. Two generators hummed to life and within seconds a blue arc covered the fence in both directions. The corpses who had their peeling fingers entwined in the chain links began to shake and twist, dust flying from their hair and clothes. Thompson watched as the ones far enough away from the fence to be spared began to back up. They were at least smart enough to have some sense of self-preservation left. When the masses began to move away, Thompson let go of the red button, and the generators fell silent. He cut the alarm as well.

Those bodies which had been caught against the fence ceased their jerking and fell backwards, some of them breaking into pieces on impact with the ground. A couple remained hanging from the chain links, smoldering. The smell of cooking, rancid meat hit their nostrils causing one of the men to lean over and vomit into the dust.

Thompson looked out at the retreating hordes and then to Jared. "Check on him," he cocked a thumb toward the heaving soldier. Jared went instantly, his eyes still wide from his first firefight.

Thompson then turned his attention to their guest, who had dismounted his horse and was trying to calm the beast.

The stranger looked up at Thompson's approach. He held out a hand. "Thank you."

Thompson looked at the hand a moment before taking it. The action surprised him. "You're welcome," he replied. He watched the stranger stroke the horse's neck for a moment or two more before continuing. "I'm Sergeant Thompson."

"Monroe," the stranger replied.

Thompson released the newcomer's hand, taking a moment to note the firm grip. "Forgive us if we seem caught flat-footed, Mr. Monroe, but we haven't gotten a visitor in a long time."

Monroe smiled. "No mister necessary, sergeant. Monroe will do nicely by itself." He scanned the now hundreds of corpses milling about beyond the fence. "I can see why your city's not a tourist attraction." He sighed and lowered his voice. "Are you in charge here, sergeant?"

"Please," Thompson replied, "Thompson is fine by itself as well. No titles necessary."

"Agreed," Monroe smiled. "But are you?"

Thompson shook his head just as the Mayor arrived, red-faced. "As I live and breathe, a visitor!" Without warning, the Mayor embraced the much taller Monroe, making for a very comical scene.

Monroe looked to Thompson as if for assistance, but Thompson had none to give. He merely smiled and half-shrugged.

The Mayor released Monroe and shook hands forcibly. "It's been a long time, my friend. I'm the Mayor of this city. And you are?"

Monroe introduced himself much the same way he had with Thompson.

"I see," the Mayor mused aloud. "And what can you tell us? Do you have any news?"

Monroe's brow furrowed and he glanced behind him to the men and women collecting themselves by the fence. One of the women was casually reloading shells into her shotgun. He then looked past the Mayor to the citizens gathering just inside the inner perimeter. Thompson saw Sally with her small class standing a few yards back. Monroe pitched his voice low again. "Mr. Mayor, I believe I have news that would best be delivered to yourself and Thompson here alone."

The Mayor nodded gravely. "I understand." He turned to Thompson. "Put things to rights here, would you Thompson? I'll get the Commander and we can meet at my office in a few minutes."

Thompson nodded. "All right."

The Mayor then took Monroe by the arm and led him in the direction of the municipal building. As they passed through the crowd, the Mayor commented to everyone, "It's all right, folks. You can go back to your business, the emergency has passed and everything is fine. Go on, now."

Thompson watched them go with a vague feeling of unease. He turned to the men and women still recovering from the firefight. Other than the woman with the shotgun, they seemed out of breath and uncertain of what to do next. Few had ever fired their guns before. Jared, wild-eyed and in a state of seeming shock, looked to Thompson for guidance.

"All right," Thompson cleared his throat, "those of you on watch, back to your post. Those not on watch, back inside. Thames," he indicated the woman with the shotgun, "take my spot. I need to go inside and see what's up with our visitor."

Thames spoke up. "Should we double the watch, sergeant?"

He considered this. "No, Thames, I don't think that's a good idea. Too much attention already." He jerked a thumb at the outer perimeter. Beyond the chain links were their constant wardens. None of them seemed concerned with their fallen comrades, the meat there too stale for their tastes. The majority of the figures outside simply stood and stared at Thompson and associates. They would start moving aimlessly about eventually, but that could take hours.

The woman named Thames nodded and finished loading her shotgun. She moved to where Thompson had been standing and started pacing slowly back and forth.

Thompson looked to the youngest one there, Jared. He still seemed to be piloting his body by remote control. "Jared," Thompson said.

Jared took too long to answer. "Yes. Yes, sir?"

"Are you all right?"

Jared nodded quickly.

"Take a rest, Jared," Thompson put a hand on the young man's shoulder. "Seriously."

Jared nodded again and wandered inside the perimeter. He did so with a vague sense of loss following him.

Thompson watched him go. He turned to the two men remaining. Everyone else had gone back to their posts as ordered. "Murphy, take Jared's shift. Coleman, go after him and make sure he's okay."

They nodded and did as he bade them.

Thompson sighed and looked through the fence to the outside world once more. Toward the back, the crowd began to thin, as they seemed to forget why they were there. At the gate, a mere two feet from the links, a young girl in what looked to be her Sunday dress stood amongst the bodies and stared inhumanly at him. Her rheumy eyes were locked onto his.

He shuddered despite himself. *A child*, he thought. *A child into this world.*

Thompson remembered Sally, and turned to where she had been standing with her students. She was gone, however. No doubt she had left once it was clear the danger had past to get her children away from the bodies. And the smell.

He walked inside the perimeter and down Main Street. Two blocks later he was at what had been the elementary school. He made his way to the window of Sally's classroom and looked inside. She appeared to be lecturing them about something, perhaps what they just witnessed. They had seen worse, he knew. Many of them lost parents on the way here; most of them were orphans. So few children left.

His thoughts went back to the undead girl whose eyes so easily found him. *So few* live *ones*, he thought dismally.

Sally looked up and saw him through the window. She paused in her speech and raised her eyebrows questioningly. *Is everything all right?* she was asking him.

He nodded his answer. She returned to her address quickly, so as not to call attention to the soldier outside. No sense exciting the children any more than they already were. He walked away from the school and toward the municipal building. Time to find out what the newcomer had to say.

Thompson walked up the stairs and turned when he reached the front door. He looked up and down the parts of Main Street that he could see. Deserted completely. *Less than ninety people in the City, Thompson*, he explained to himself. *You can't expect teeming masses with only ninety people.*

Best get to work on that, he half-joked.

He closed his eyes. That wasn't funny at all.

Thompson opened the front door and walked inside. He made his way to the Mayor's office. The Mayor himself was behind his desk and The Commander sat in one of the chairs, sipping coffee. The latter nodded to Thompson upon his entrance.

Monroe had taken off his wide-brimmed hat and left the rest of his black garments on. He stood by the door with his arms crossed, looking grave. Once Thompson had come into the room, the taller man seemed to become animate once more. "I hope the both of you know that this man saved my life," he said with as close an emotion to cheer as he seemed capable of mustering. He took Thompson's hand and shook it, although more excitedly than he had done a few minutes back.

The Commander finally spoke with pride in his voice, as if he had been responsible for Thompson's expertise. "Thompson's our best man out there, Mr. Monroe."

Monroe did not correct The Commander on his desire to not have a title. He acted as if it did not matter. Thompson went to the other side of the door and leaned against the wall much as Monroe had done. He did not feel like sitting.

The Mayor adjusted himself behind his desk. "So...Monroe, tell us this important news."

Monroe's face became grim once more. "I will. I came from McMurtrie."

The Commander straightened in his chair. "Fort McMurtrie? But why did you ride all that way? They came by helicopter the last two times—"

Monroe shook his head sadly. "There is no 'they' anymore, Commander."

The room fell silent for several moments.

Thompson broke in finally. "So the base fell."

Monroe simply nodded.

"Impossible!" The Commander nearly knocked his chair over when he stood. "They were even more fortified than the City is! They had a good portion of their garrison intact! It's impossible, I tell you."

"Impossible," Monroe repeated after a moment. "Not too long ago, Commander, if I had walked in here and told you that the dead were getting back up and coming after the living, you would have said 'impossible' then, too."

The Commander could not reply.

"Regardless," the man continued, "don't take my word for it. Try raising them on your radio. I know they spoke with you at least once a week. Try calling them."

The Mayor's head drooped. "We have been. Nothing."

Monroe looked from The Mayor to The Commander as if his point had been proved.

The Commander hummed in his throat for a moment. "At least tell me how."

"Internal problems," Monroe answered. "There were arguments, the base broke down into factions. These factions warred with each other. At first just roughhousing, really. Then someone started using guns. The perimeter was breached while they were otherwise engaged in killing each other. Then the dead came in and finished it."

The Commander shook his head. "I don't understand. Colonel Roberts had that post, and that doesn't sound like him at all."

Monroe almost smirked. "Strange times do things to a man."

The Commander still seemed unable to comprehend the news. "I don't understand. I've seen McMurtrie. How could they have gotten through their defenses?"

Monroe smiled. "Well, I must admit—we did help them." Then the man moved.

There was a blur, a movement in the air that no one could fathom. Within seconds, a gunshot filled the small room with ringing ears.

The Commander lolled back in his chair, a neat hole in his forehead, what had been the back of his head now sliding down the wall behind him. To his credit, he had tried to draw his own sidearm upon hearing the words "I must admit." It hung from his lifeless index finger, the muzzle touching the floor.

Monroe stood over him with one of his pistols in hand, the barrel smoking.

Thompson remained where he was, too shocked to do anything else.

Surprisingly enough, it was The Mayor who moved next. He scrambled to the floor and went on all fours toward the Commander's gun. Under his breath, he muttered, "Oh God, Oh God, Oh God…"

Thompson at that point began to move and Monroe turned his pistol toward him. "Wait," he told Monroe. "Don't!" He dove toward the Mayor.

The Mayor, despite his size, was crawling very fast, powered by fright. He grabbed the Commander's sidearm and stood up, bringing it to rest in both hands, pointed straight at Monroe. "Y-You—" He could not seem to finish his thought.

Thompson found himself on the floor behind the Mayor. He had badly anticipated the large man's speed and missed completely. "Mayor—"

Monroe lowered his own gun and seemed about to reassure Thompson. "It's all right, Thompson—"

The Commander's sidearm roared twice and Monroe jerked with each impact. He stumbled backwards into the wall by the door, staining it with his blood. He hung there for a moment, leaning against it as if he had been hit with a sudden fainting spell.

The gun went limp in the Mayor's hands, as if he could not believe what he had just done.

Thompson had to admit he would have never thought it possible himself. "Mr. Mayor," he began, but Monroe interrupted him.

"I was going to say," the man said, standing up and brushing himself off, "that they always try that. With the same results."

Thompson took a moment to assure himself that yes, Monroe had just taken two bullets in the chest and was talking to him calmly as if to discuss the weather. Then he very quickly disarmed the Mayor.

The Mayor bemoaned the loss of his weapon and cowered behind Thompson. "But the gun!" he protested.

"Won't do you any good," Thompson told the man.

Monroe smiled. His former gloom was gone. "You're very astute, my friend. I respect that."

"I saw how you can move," Thompson said coldly, "so I knew we were fucked."

Monroe laughed. "No, no, you've got it all wrong."

Thompson shook his head. "I don't got it at all, Monroe, wrong or otherwise. You're not one of them. They don't talk and ride horses."

"They don't need guns either," Monroe added. "Neither do I, but it sometimes makes it easier."

"Easier?" The Mayor seemed to peep from behind Thompson.

Thompson gestured for the Mayor to keep quiet. "All right. Fine. I give up. What the hell are you?"

Monroe stepped in front of them toward the Commander's body. "Excuse me. I can't wait any longer for this," he said simply, and bent over the corpse. He opened his mouth wide and bit down into the Commander's neck.

Thompson heard the Mayor give out a small scream from behind him and felt the man bury his face into the back of his jacket. Although he was of the opinion the Mayor had the right idea, he could not seem to look away.

Blood coursed down the Commander's chest and dangling arm, though not much. Monroe had clamped down onto the neck and was sucking the majority of the liquid down his throat. His eyes were closed and he held on to the body with both hands to keep it steady.

Thompson was not sure how long had passed before Monroe finally finished and stood up. The body slumped further in the chair. He wiped some spare blood from his chin. He looked at Thompson and smiled. "You and I need to talk."

"Yes, I think we do," Thompson replied.

Thompson turned to face the Mayor; the man's face was red and his teeth were grinding together. Thompson thought it was bad enough to try to get used to the idea that you had shot a man. Certainly not helping matters was the fact the man seemed to shake it off and find the whole affair humorous. "Get out," he told the Mayor. "Tell everyone else that comes running to stay out until I say so."

The Mayor nodded quickly and did not have to be told twice. He went out the door and slammed it shut behind him.

Monroe sat down in the chair next to the Commander and waited for Thompson to speak.

Thompson sat down on the rim of the Mayor's desk and looked at their guest. His chest had two starbursts of dark crimson that became black once the point of impact was reached. "What are you?" Thompson asked involuntarily.

Monroe smiled and spread out his hands. "You don't know?"

Thompson thought for a moment and closed his eyes. "I can't accept that." His mind raced. "No, you see—I've seen the movies—"

"They're mostly wrong."

"You have to be invited in," Thompson accused.

"You did." Monroe cleared his throat and yelled, "Come on, get in here!" in a voice that sounded eerily like Thompson's own.

Thompson's eyes widened and he sat back further on the desk. He felt the room spin just for a second.

"Neat trick, eh?" Monroe asked, leaning forward.

Thompson put his forehead into his hand and closed his eyes. "It's overcast today, so the sun wouldn't bother you."

"It itches, though," Monroe added. "Between the clouds and the clothing, it's passable."

"And the horse. You used the horse to ride in on because you knew they wouldn't want you. They wanted something warm."

Monroe nodded. "Because, well, I'm dead, too." He pointed at Thompson. "You're good. We're going to get along fine."

Thompson shook his head. "This. This is unreal."

"Come on, Thompson. It's not that big a stretch once you accept zombies to accept vampires." Monroe paused. "And why Thompson? Why can't I call you by your first name?"

Thompson closed his eyes. "So I killed him."

Monroe leaned forward. "What? Killed who?" He pointed at The Commander's lifeless form. "Him?"

Thompson nodded.

"Listen," Monroe leaned forward and put a hand on the man's knee. "You've seen what I can do. I would have gotten in one way or another. If not you, someone else. Trust me."

Thompson flinched involuntarily from the man's touch. It felt like any other man's. "You've done this before."

Monroe nodded.

"You did this at McMurtrie."

Again, a nod.

Thompson sighed. "So what happens now? You kill me?"

Monroe stood up and stretched, his spine crackling. "Why would I want to kill you, Thompson?"

Thompson cut his eyes to the body of The Commander. "Why did you kill him?"

"An example," Monroe responded quickly. "I needed to let you know what I could do."

"So why wasn't I the example?" Thompson asked. "Why not The Mayor?"

Monroe shrugged. "The Mayor didn't look like something I would want to drink. And you—you saved my horse and let me in. And you're quick. I need you alive."

Thompson frowned. "I don't understand. Why am I special? What makes me different from the people at McMurtrie you murdered?"

Monroe walked over to the window and looked out. He turned and smiled. "Cooperation."

"With?"

"Our plan. It's very simple really. Would you like to hear it?"

Do I have a choice? Thompson almost asked, but thought better of it. He simply nodded.

Monroe began pacing as he spoke. "Basically, you humans are ridiculous creatures." He stopped as if to correct himself. "I say that as one who has been a human and gotten over it." He resumed walking. "The entire world is covered with the undead—" He pointed to the window. "—*that* kind of undead, I mean—and what do you do? You squabble amongst yourselves over who's in charge. You stake your claim on property and money as if they still meant something. You spent most of your time back when this could have been stopped trying to decide who was to blame instead of solving the problem." He sighed. "Typical.

"So what do you have now? You have billions of undead and you're outnumbered. You've retreated to military bases and walled-in cities and you're trying to figure out what to do next. If you just waited long enough, they'd rot to the point where they were immobile and you could walk through the streets shooting and burning them. But we've decided you won't make it that long. You'll kill each other off before they have the chance."

Thompson stood up. "We? Who is we? There's more than just you?"

Monroe smiled. "Oh, yes. Lots more than just me."

"So what is it all of you have decided about all of us mere humans?" Thompson asked, unable to get the sarcastic edge out of his voice.

"Why, we've decided to help keep you alive of course."

Thompson blinked. "Alive?"

"Yes, alive," Monroe walked across the room toward the desk. "Don't go dense on me now, Thompson. We can't drink blood once they're that far gone. It has to be a recent kill." He nodded to The Commander. "Like him.

"So naturally we want to find the strongholds of you humans and keep you alive and breeding."

Thompson looked up at him. "So you can feed off of us and keep yourselves alive."

Monroe smiled and nodded. "See, I told you you were the bright one of the bunch." He started pacing again. "We can ensure that you'll survive. For the most part, you won't even notice we're here."

Thompson laughed. "Except for the holes in our necks."

"A small price to pay," Monroe shrugged. "Others have gotten used to that minor inconvenience."

"Others?" Thompson raised an eyebrow. "How many others?"

"A few thousand," Monroe replied, as if it were nothing. "They liked the idea of being able to continue their way of life."

Thompson crossed his arms and thought for several moments. "What if we kill you instead?"

Monroe looked amused.

"What if we were able to kill you instead? We could hold you at bay with crosses till one of us could stake you."

Monroe burst out laughing. "No offense, my friend—but in a world like this it's hard to imagine that God exists now. Or maybe that he ever did exist to begin with." He seemed to calm himself. "No, you could probably pull that off. You're a resourceful young guy. But if I don't report back to the rest of the group that you've agreed, they'll come in here and kill you all. They'll kill all of you, drain you dry, and then demolish the fence and let the zombies in."

Thompson's brow creased. He considered this for a full minute. "And if we simply say no?"

Monroe's smile became very cold. "Then the same thing happens. Only I'm still here and I'll help them take this place apart." He nodded. "I don't think you want that, Thompson. I think you want to live. I think you have someone to live for."

Thompson looked startled.

"No, I can't read your mind, Thompson," Monroe laughed again. "I just saw the way you and the schoolteacher looked at each other. At least, I assume she's a schoolteacher; she was with those children."

Thompson smirked despite himself. "So you're here to save us all."

"And ourselves. We're very selfish creatures, make no mistake."

Thompson leaned back on the desk. "So I really have no choice to make, do I?"

Monroe shook his head. "I'm sorry, Thompson. You may not believe that, but it's true. It seems like if you were running this place it would all work out for the best without us. But we can't take that risk. We go hungry without the living, so the living must be kept that way—living.

"I've seen too many human settlements crumble due to internal strife. It cannot be allowed any longer."

Thompson nodded.

"What is your first name anyway?" Monroe asked.

Thompson shook his head. "It doesn't matter. Listen, suppose I say yes to this. What happens to us?"

Monroe smiled. "Nothing. Not really, anyway. You're allowed to continue as you have been. Only we're in charge and we'll come by whenever we want. And feed whenever we want. On whomever we want." He directed this last part at Thompson.

Thompson stiffened.

"That's right. Even your schoolteacher."

Thompson drew his own gun and pointed it at the other man's forehead. This was all accomplished in one swift motion that seemed only slightly slower than Monroe's had been minutes before. Monroe did not even blink.

"Thompson, what are you doing?" He asked plainly. "Tell me

exactly what you think you're doing. Because, well—I'm very curious to know."

Thompson's breathing was ragged. "If you touch her—" he began.

"What?" Monroe taunted. "If I touch her, what? Do you think this is a sexual thing, Thompson? Do you think I *want* your schoolteacher? You *have* been watching too many movies. Your blood is food to me, Thompson, nothing else."

Thompson's trigger finger twitched. "My Sally is not your damn food, Monroe."

"So what are you going to do, Thompson? Shoot me?" Monroe smirked. "We've already seen what the end result of that is. It will just mean that your Sally is not anybody's food but the zombies.'"

Thompson closed his eyes. His head seemed to shake from side to side of its own accord.

"Besides, I wouldn't want to drink from 'your' Sally."

"What?" Thompson's eyes snapped open. "What did you just say?"

Monroe shook his head in pity. "First you don't want me to drink from her and now you're offended that I'm not going to." He paused a moment. "I can't drink from her because she's pregnant, Thompson. I assume it must be your child."

The gun in Thompson's hands lowered itself. "She's—" he stopped. "She's—"

Monroe frowned. "You don't know? Well, she may not know yet herself. She's not very far along. I can't drink from her because I don't know what that will do to the child, and children are obviously very important to us."

The gun was now pointing at the floor. "But we—we were—"

"Being careful?" Monroe asked. "You know there's only one one-hundred-percent effective form of birth control, Thompson."

Thompson sat down heavily on the side of the desk, his head reeling. "Sally—" he began, and then stopped. He could not seem to speak. "But how did you—?"

"No mind reading there, either," Monroe explained. "I see things...differently than you do, Thompson. Where one living being should be standing there's another inside her. It's hard to explain but easy for me to see."

Monroe took a step toward him and put a hand on his shoulder. He sighed. "Let me guess. You love her, she loves you. You weren't sure about bringing a child into a world ruled by the dead. But now—"

Thompson laughed despite himself, tears standing out in his eyes. "But now I don't know whether to be happy or not. God, this is all so fucked up!" He pounded a fist against the desk.

Monroe sighed. "Look at it this way, Thompson. We're here and it's in our best interests to keep humanity going through this. It might take a long time, but we'll get there. There's just going to be some trying times until then."

"And then?" Thompson wiped at his eyes. "When they're gone, and it's only humans and vampires again. What then?"

Monroe stopped. "To be honest, we've never considered it. Let's just say that at that time, we'll renegotiate."

Thompson nodded. He felt utterly defeated. There only seemed to be one thing left on his mind. "Does...does it hurt?" He opened his eyes to see Monroe standing virtually on top of him.

"Only for a second," Monroe reassured him. "But first, you have to tell me what your first name is."

Thompson smiled. "It's Eugene. That's why everyone calls me Thompson." He considered for a moment. "Why do you want to be called Monroe?"

"Francis," Monroe stated. "My first name is Francis. I know how you feel."

Monroe leaned into Thompson and the soldier closed his eyes. He kept seeing Sally, months from now, her belly swollen with their child. And then if she's pregnant again, he thought madly, they won't touch her. If she can just stay pregnant...

He hardly noticed the pain until it was already over.

Kora

My name is Thomas Munford, and I remember a time when my life was sane and normal. You must understand that I was never one for run-ins with ghosts or vampires. I would have never been in a story in the *Universal Tribune*, the end-all be-all of tabloids. I have never, to my knowledge, been abducted by aliens. I have never been able to bend silverware on a whim. As I said, everything in my world was perfectly average and everyday.

I went to work in the morning at an advertising agency, I went out with some friends in the office for lunch, I went home. I went home to my loving almost-fiancée, and we were happy. One of us would cook dinner, we would sit in front of the television and eat, and then we would go back into the bedroom and perform some… satisfactory lovemaking.

Sane, right? Perfectly normal, right?

Well, it was sane and perfectly normal until April 2, 1993, when I came home to a dark apartment and found the note.

You have to understand: after having such an incredibly normal life for twenty-eight years, I sometimes wondered whether all of the bizarre, all of the abnormal, all of the…well, weirdness that I was supposed to have in my life would someday show up on my doorstep and say, "Mr. Munford? It seems you're overdue for some strange, obtuse phenomena. With interest. Sign here please."

Well, on April 2, 1993, it did just that.

The note was from Linda. It said that she had been picked up at the restaurant where she was a hostess by a member of some obscure European nation's royalty. At first it had been just a drink or two, and then they went to dinner, and then they had decided that they were madly in love with one another. She had come back here to gather her things and leave the note. *Love*, she signed it. *Love, Linda.*

Well, I was somewhat less than pleased at this turn of events, as you should imagine. To be perfectly honest, I had never heard of this particular European country, even though I do fairly well in the geography category on game shows. I wandered into a bookstore a couple of days afterward and picked up an almanac.

Turns out the gross national product of that country was less than what she normally made in a year at her hosting job.

Linda never did very well in the geography category on game shows.

So, I took a part-time job to take care of my emotional woes. It didn't pay very well, but it kept me busy. It was called Professional Moping.

This lasted for about three months or so, until my friends at work felt that my part-time job was interfering with my full-time one. One Friday after work, I was standing at the water cooler, minding my own business...then they ambushed me. They dragged me out to their car, threw me in and informed me we were going to a nightclub. They told me it was one of their favorites, and they knew I would love it.

I had deadlines, but they refused to listen. I tried to explain to them that I had stacks of moping back at the apartment that had to get done, but they would have none of it. They told me I really had no choice in the matter.

Recognizing I was outnumbered, I made it clear that I would go, yes, but only under protest.

Duly noted, they said, and pulled into the parking lot of the Pick Up Styx Club, where Styx was spelled like that band from the eighties.

We paid a ridiculous cover charge, got a table and sat. After my companions tried in vain to get me out on the dance floor, or to have a drink, or to...well, do something to let them know that I was actually there and breathing, they became frustrated and left me to my fate there at the table.

So there I was, minding my own business, at a table in the Pick Up Styx Club, when I happened to see a woman sitting at a table across the room. She appeared to have the same predicament as myself—being alone. She was not just any woman, either, but an incredibly beautiful woman. Not the kind you see on television, those ones who are so amazingly perfect that you just know they had to have been grown in some laboratory. She was just...beautiful.

I heard one time that if you try to describe a woman and you simply can't, then she must be beautiful, indeed. So remember that and just trust me when I tell you that she was something else.

I figured that since she was alone, and I was alone, maybe we could be alone together. Maybe we even had similar part-time jobs and could compare notes.

With this in mind, I walked up to her table and asked her whether or not the chair next to her was taken.

She looked at it, almost comically, as though confirming there was no one sitting there. She told me it was available.

I sat down; I noticed that she had the most amazing green eyes. They seemed to look right into me.

"You look like you feel about as out of place as I do," I said.

She laughed. "This is my first time here," she explained.

"Mine, too. I got dragged here by some friends."

"I came alone," she replied. "The name caught my attention."

"You like eighties music?" I asked.

"Something like that," she said and smiled.

The eyes set me up for the kill, but her smile finished me off. "Would you like to go somewhere else, get a bite to eat or something?" I asked.

She looked around us, and then shrugged. "Why not?"

She waited by the front door while I went to tell my coworkers that I was leaving. Before I had taken five steps away from her, one of them saw me, looked at her, and waved me on furiously. Apparently, he approved.

We took her car as I had arrived as a prisoner. We found one of those twenty-four-hour pancake emporiums and had breakfast. Her name was Kora, and she was born on the island of Sicily, of all places. She had stayed in Europe for most of her life and had emigrated to the States recently because she wanted something new in her life. We talked through two pots of coffee, and she invited me back to her place.

The first thing I noticed about her apartment—apart from the den being the size of my entire place—was that she owned more plants than anyone I had ever met before. Plants of all shapes and sizes were on the entertainment center, on the end tables, hanging from hooks in the corners of the room—everywhere.

We sat there in the den, surrounded by foliage, and talked until it was nearly dawn.

Finally, I felt that all the coffee I had consumed needed to be dealt with, so I asked her where her facilities were. When I came back, she was curled up in a ball on the loveseat and sound asleep. I took the afghan off the back of the seat, covered her up with it and sat down in a chair. I, too, fell asleep soon afterward.

When I awoke sometime around noon, she was sitting up on the loveseat and watching me. I asked her what she was looking at. She told me she was looking at me.

"Why didn't you leave after I fell asleep?" she asked.

"No way to lock the door behind me," I told her.

She nodded. After a moment, she said, "You didn't try to get me into the bedroom all last night. Why?"

"I outgrew one-night stands a while back," I said, "and I figured that if it was going to be more than that, then time would tell."

She nodded. After another moment, she said, "Why didn't you at least lie down on the bed? It's more comfortable than that chair."

"I don't feel right about sleeping on anybody else's bed without being invited."

At this, she got up off the loveseat and offered me her hand. "I'm inviting you now," she said.

We went into her bedroom and performed some lovemaking that was…much better than satisfactory. Much better, indeed.

That evening she drove me back to my apartment. "One last thing," she said, and pulled from out of her purse a key. "Now you can lock the door behind you."

I told her she really didn't know me very well, at least not enough to be giving me a key to her apartment.

She said, "Oh, I know you better than you think, Thomas."

I told her that I was really looking for something solid, not just a string of one-night stands.

She said, "I know," and then she kissed me again. "I'm looking for that myself."

I got out of her car and she drove off. She waved out the window at me as she passed. I felt numb. In the space of one evening, I had found the woman of my dreams. She was funny, she was incredibly beautiful and sexy, she listened to what I had to say, she didn't get offended if I decided to breathe or something else equally silly, and well, she knew how to use her body in ways that I had not previously encountered.

Our relationship grew over the next couple of months, and it was frightening to both of us how well things were working out. We would go to movies, we would go to the park, or just sit at home and talk. It was wonderful.

The guys at work were happy, too. I had come back from the dead, or so they claimed, and I must admit it was easier to get things done in the office when life was good outside the office.

At times I wanted to pinch myself to see whether I would wake up, but I shouldn't have worried. One day, something did pinch me, and I woke up hard.

It was near the end of November; Kora disappeared.

I called her apartment for a few days, and the answering machine picked up every single time.

I couldn't try her at the office; she said she didn't have a job.

I finally used my key to look in at her apartment. She was not there either. Everything was still in its place, so she must have left in a hurry. All the plants were in various stages of death.

I scribbled a note on a piece of paper. I left it on the kitchen table where she couldn't help but see it and then went home.

I lost sleep, I didn't feel like eating, and I kept telling myself over and over again, *You idiot! You idiot! You went and did it again, didn't you? Got involved and were surprised when it blew up in your face!*

In-between these bouts of berating myself, in my more collected moments, I would try to dissect the situation in a logical manner. Nothing about it made any sense. Why would she leave everything in her apartment as though she meant to come back? Why leave me with a key to it when she knew she'd be gone? There couldn't be two people from the same obscure European nation trawling for wives in this city, could there?

That first week, I went by Kora's apartment every day after work. I wanted to see if the note had moved at all, certain that if she stopped by her apartment, even for a moment, she would have at least picked it up.

At one point, I walked in and found the note gone. I began calling out her name, suddenly positive she was in her bedroom. This notion lasted for all of thirty seconds, which was the time it took for me to realize that the gust of air I created by opening the apartment door had blown the note off the table.

Fear gripped me then, and I began to suspect foul play. The surety struck me like a bus. She had been kidnapped, of course! That explained everything! I would go straight to the police and start the wheels of justice turning!

With exclamation points bouncing around in my mind, and my legs taking me sprinting out the door, I almost barreled right over Kora's landlady. "Where are you going in such a hurry, young man?" she asked me.

"Your tenant, the one who lives in this apartment, Kora—she's gone missing," I said quickly, knowing that every second I wasted there was another the kidnappers had on their side. "I'm going to the police."

"She hasn't gone missing, you silly man," the woman said, wagging a finger in my face. "Every year at this time she asks me to hold her mail, and she takes a trip back home. She's back around the end of March."

"She went to Sicily?" I asked her, but she shook her head.

"I don't pry into my tenants' business, which is why I'm going to forget she made a copy of her key for you." She smiled and walked away, admonishing lightly, "Go home and get some sleep. You look like you could use it."

With my sudden need to visit the local precinct deflated, I tried to do as she advised me, but it would be a long time before I slept well again.

That winter was the longest I have ever suffered through. I worked like a madman, got promoted, but still kept going. They had to throw me out every night, because I never wanted to go home. Christmas was terrible; I didn't even bother to put up my bachelor's edition no-muss-no-fuss-plastic-three-foot tree. It seemed pointless. New Year's, I stayed home. I wouldn't answer the door or my phone because I knew that it was just my friends from work, trying to get me involved with someone else who would ruin my life. Valentine's Day, I got drunk. I went to the liquor store, restocked my cabinet, and drank all night long. I called in sick the next day and lay in bed, miserable with a hangover that would have made angels weep and devils take notes.

March finally arrived. Every day after work I went to her apartment to sit in the chair I had fallen asleep in that first night. The end of March, the landlady had said, but maybe she had been wrong, or maybe Kora would get back early, or maybe...I don't really know what I was thinking. I knew I just wanted to hear Kora's story, then walk out of her life forever. I have never been awash with such a mixture of love, hate and confusion before.

On the morning of March 22, I woke up and found Kora sitting on the loveseat across from me, just as she had that first night. For a brief moment, I wondered whether I had dreamed the last four months.

"You're here," she said.

"So are you," I said back.

Neither of us said anything for either several minutes or several years—it was hard to tell which.

"Go ahead," I offered finally.

She looked confused. "Go ahead and what?"

"Tell me why you left and didn't tell me where you were going," I said. "Tell me, so I can go home."

Her eyes searched the floor. "I knew you would be upset."

"Well, Christ, Kora," I almost yelled, "what am I supposed to be? Tell me, so I can leave."

She sighed. "You're not going to believe me."

"That remains to be seen," I replied.

"All right," she said, then said it again, "all right. You'll be sorry you asked, most likely." She waited for an interruption from me, and when she didn't get one, she said, "Kora is my real name, but it's not the one you probably know me by."

"What do you mean?" I asked, "It's the only name you've ever told me you had."

"Does the name Prosperina ring a bell?"

"No, no, it doesn't."

"Okay, look, I'm royalty. Sort of. From a place...below here."

"What, Australia?" I asked.

"Look," she said, exasperated, "do I have to spell out for you?

I'm the Queen of the Underworld, all right? I didn't want to be, but years ago my dad made a deal with the King, got me dragged down there, and before I knew it, I had eaten some fruit and I was stuck! I didn't want to leave you, but I had no choice!"

She stared at me like I was stupid or something.

I stared back like she was having a psychotic break or something.

"What?" I asked.

"You heard me. My more popular name is Persephone, and I am the Queen of the Underworld. Hades is my husband, or Pluto, whichever you prefer. And Zeus was, is, my father—or Jupiter, whichever you prefer. They only had two names, one Greek and one Roman, to confuse schoolchildren, I think.

"Anyway, about a month before the winter solstice, I have to go back down into the Underworld, and I get to come back after the vernal equinox. I have to, I have no choice."

At that point I did what I think any other red-blooded American male would do.

I started laughing uncontrollably.

I was surprised I didn't break the chair I was sitting in. Between laughs I managed to tell her that that was the most original excuse I had ever heard, and it almost made it worth the wait through the winter to hear it.

Kora, however, was not laughing.

I finally calmed down, and studied her face. "You're not laughing," I said.

"No," she said, obviously fuming, "I am not."

"You really...I mean, you don't seriously believe what you just told me, do you?"

She continued to look at me, fury behind her green eyes.

I got up and began backing toward the door. "Whoa, whoa, whoa," I said. "Look, I really like you and all, but I seem to have this allergic reaction to people that are out of their minds."

"I'm not crazy, Thomas," she said, following me.

We faced each other, and at that point a lightbulb clicked on in my head. Some literature class somewhere or something came to the fore. "*Now* I remember the goddess you're talking about. You're telling me that you're her."

"Yes, that is exactly what I'm telling you."

"So you're telling me that because you go down into this Underworld of yours every year in November, the leaves fall off the trees, the days get shorter, the seasons change, and it gets colder. Is that what you're telling me?"

"Don't be stupid!" she spat out. "Any idiot knows that happens because the earth tilts away from the sun so that less solar radiation hits the northern hemisphere. It has nothing to do with me! Back then, they had no clue about any of that, so they put the blame on me and the other fertility goddesses. None of us are very happy about it; I mean, it doesn't even make any sense! How do you explain the summer in the southern hemisphere while I'm gone? And when you try to explain it to anyone, what do they do? Kneel and offer libations! Damn silly and annoying."

While she spoke, she absent-mindedly turned to the fern on the table and touched it on one of its brown and withered leaves. Since I had a key, I don't know why I hadn't tried to perform some upkeep on the poor things. I guess I had been so depressed it never crossed my mind. Anyway, she touched this plant, and it...I don't know...started to glow a bit, and within seconds it was a happy and healthy fern again.

She stopped and looked up at me. I thank God that I will never have to know what the look on my face was like at that particular moment.

"What?" She asked, when she saw whatever strange configuration my face was manifesting. She followed my gaze to the rejuvenated fern, and then looked back. "Oh, that. That's one of the side effects of being out of your mind."

"I need to sit down now," I said. "Right...now." I meant it, too. I felt my legs starting to give way, so she pulled out a chair and let me give way into it.

She sat down next to me.

After a few minutes of looking from her to the plant and back again, I finally said, "You weren't kidding."

"No."

"And you're not a lunatic."

"I don't think so, no."

"You're really Persephone."

"Yes," she said. "That's what most of the books call me, but I prefer Kora, which is what I was before Hades came and snatched me up."

"And he's your husband? What, is he going to come looking for me, or something?"

"Yes, well, we're separated."

I shook my head. "I don't understand any of this."

"Hold on," she said, "I'll explain. Do you want something to drink first?"

"Will I need it?"

She assessed my mental health at that moment. "I think so."

"Good. Yes. I would like something."

She mixed a couple of drinks and brought them back to the table.

"Okay, you understand the story, right? It's pretty much accurate. I sat at the side of my husband, the King, for a while, even got into the royalty bit. Held court. Stuff like that. I even started hanging out in the Underworld year-round. Nobody bothered with the spring festivals any more. Even back then, they had gotten too commercialized. After a couple of hundred years, though, it got boring. For both of us. And then, the Shift happened."

"Shift?"

"Yes, the Shift. Everyone found new religions to keep them occupied, and they didn't need us any more. The souls incoming finally dwindled to nothing, and the place stagnated. Oh, we still ruled over the ones that were there, but finally Hades kind of gave up. He sits down there and broods about his lost kingdom. I tried to comfort him, I mean, I was his wife, but finally one day I decided that I had had enough. I thought to myself, 'If I hear Sisyphus rolling that stone one more time, I shall simply go mad.'

"I told Hades we were through, and came back up here. I wandered about for a bit, then finally settled here in the States. Every year I have to go back down, and Hades and I talk. I bring him books—something to do, you know. It's bad when you lose your will to live, especially when you're an immortal and can't die."

I nodded. I couldn't believe that I was taking it as well as I was. "So you have to go back every year?"

She nodded.

"Didn't that change because of the Shift?" I asked. "Isn't there a way out of it?"

"No, there's not a way out because there are rules," she replied, "and the rules did not change when the Shift happened."

I grasped at another idea. "Couldn't you ask your father to get you a real divorce or something? Keep you from having to leave? I don't know, something?"

"No," Kora said. "I don't know that he could do anything, but I can't even ask him because no one knows where he is. After the Shift, he went and had some angry words with the other pantheons, and then went and spoke to God."

"He spoke to God? *The* God?"

"Well, not really *the* God," she replied, "He's just *a* God, really. But He uses pseudonyms so that everyone thinks they're worshipping someone else."

"I see," I said. I think at this point I finished off my drink in one gulp.

"Anyway, no one's seen him since. I think maybe they struck a deal or something. Somebody said they saw the two of them playing golf somewhere once, but I don't know for sure. I tried to go up to The City one time and speak with one or both of them, but I kept being told by God's secretary that he was out. I asked when He was coming back, and the secretary said that He had only been gone for two hundred years this time, so it could be any year now."

"Lovely," I said.

"Tell me about it," she said, and we both laughed.

"I'm sorry I didn't believe you," I said after a moment's silence.

"I'm sorry I didn't tell you before," she said. "I never meant for you to freak out about me being gone, but I kept putting off telling you, and putting it off, and next thing I knew, I was down there hobnobbing with Charon, playing cards. He's really the only one left worth talking to, you know."

"So you and your husband...you didn't...I mean..." I trailed off. I was trying to ask a goddess whether she had had sex with her lawfully wedded husband, who was a god himself, and a god of the Underworld at that. Try that yourself and see if *you* can pull it off.

"No, the last time we did that was in the Sixth Century—A.D.— and it was such a depressing mess that we both swore never to try it again." She smiled. "I told him about you."

I blinked. "You told Hades...about me?"

"Yes, I did." She kept on smiling.

I had these lovely images in my head of me, walking to work— whistling even—when the pavement beneath me opens up, and this large, grey hand comes up from below to drag me down into the pits of eternity. I wondered whether they'd put a big A on my forehead or something.

"Well," I said, trying to remain calm, "what did he say?"

"He said," she told me, "that he was glad I was happy." She looked at my face and laughed. "And no, he's not going to come after you or anything. Or sick the Furies on you. They only do what *I* say, anyway. They don't listen to him."

"So you said you were happy."

"Yes."

"With me."

"Yes."

"And you won't sick the Harpies on me."

"Furies, darling, Furies. The Harpies are another matter entirely. And I won't let any of them touch you, as long as you keep me happy."

I thought about it for a minute, and then said, "Okay, it's a deal."

I kissed her, and she kissed me back. It was wonderful.

So anyway, that's my story. I am in love with a goddess, and yes—every November she leaves to go back down to the Underworld, and neither of us like it, but what can we do? We celebrate Christmas and Thanksgiving at the same time to avoid the problems of her missing them.

I offered to go with her, but she didn't think that would be a good idea. Mortals have a tendency not to come back, and besides, she told me, the last one who tried caused a big mess. I told her, yeah, I'll just stay here and water the plants.

I just sit here in this chair where I'm writing this now and wait for March 22, which is when she always shows up on the loveseat, and we pick up where we left off. It's not an easy way to work a relationship, eight months out of twelve, but when you think about it, most people don't even get that, so I don't complain.

This time, she said she left word for Zeus to call if he ever got back from wherever he was, hanging out with God. Maybe then, she said, she could get a real divorce from Hades, and we could get on with our lives. Have kids, she says.

That sounds better than fine to me, I said, but what am I supposed to say if he calls while you're gone? How do you address Zeus, the King of Olympus?

"Just say, 'Oh, hi Dad,'" she said. "He likes it when people call him Dad."

She smiled one of those smiles, then kissed me and left to go back to the Underworld. And unless "Dad" happens to call before then, I have to wait until March to find out whether she was joking or not.

The Last Burden

The reason Andrew had taken up hydroponics with such a lackluster attitude was that he had never really believed in it. He spent his childhood and most of his teenage years on the subsidized farms of New Mexico, working with his family in the soil. The soil was the thing he grew up with, and now he was working with everything but the soil.

However, once he had gotten over his initial displeasure at having the role of second for maintaining the food supply—and being forced to do it using these techniques—his long-cultivated farming instincts had been able to overtake his neophobia. He would never confess it to anyone else, not after his numerous and loud protestations about how "unnatural" this food was, but secretly he thought the soil-free food might actually taste better.

Andrew scanned down the inventory on his tablet, checking to make sure that everything was coming along normally. Everything was, of course. The temperature was perpetually ideal; the climate was a constant perfection. It was a plant's dream to be under Andrew's care.

He stepped to the far wall and activated the intercom. "Barbara?"

"Yes?" A woman's voice replied after a moment.
"What would you like for dinner?" He asked.
There were a few moments of silence.
"Some chicken with a little salad maybe?" He prompted. "I've got some greens down here that could have your name on them."
"That'd be great, hon," she answered.
"Okay," he said, "I'll get on it. Give me an hour, okay?"
"No problem, I'm still running some equipment checks here." There was a pause and Andrew went to step away. "Oh, and Drew?"
"Yes?"
"Have you seen California? I think it's on fire."
Andrew looked up through the window at the North American continent. She was right. Though the weather patterns were obviously clear over the western part of the land mass, a black pall seemed to have swallowed most of northern California and Oregon. "Hm, I hadn't noticed that before," he said. "Very well could be smoke."
"Oh, well," she said, signing off. "See you in an hour."
Andrew took one last look out the window before returning to the garden.

It had taken Andrew six weeks to stop dreaming about the man with the ravaged, bloody face.

Andrew's primary function on the mission had been communications, so he was manning his post when the last transmission came through.

Even after all the screaming had stopped, there had been some signals coming to them from Earth. A civil service station in Miami was still broadcasting their empty desk and a background littered with bodies. A television channel out of Barcelona had a screen up that stated what Andrew was pretty sure said, "Technical Difficulties, Please Stand By." A disc jockey at some AM station had, with questionable taste, left an endless loop of "Stairway to Heaven" going.

For the most part, though, people with transmitters had the decency to shut them off before laying down to die. Either that, or power grids had failed quickly with no living human eyes to monitor them.

Andrew had been watching one of the twenty-four-hour news channels specifically because they had been bound and determined to report everything until the very end...and appeared to have succeeded. For two hours, Andrew sat, unmoving, watching the empty newsroom. For two hours, all he perceived was the odd groan and the sound of someone shuffling around off camera.

Finally, the author of the noises came into view. He was dressed in camouflage pants and a T-shirt; his long stringy blond hair obscured his face. His unkempt nature was too much for a news anchor, even in these end times. Andrew figured he was a cameraman or engineer of some sort.

The man bumped into the desk and stopped. His splotched hands came forward and inspected the obstacle; his fingernails making small scratching sounds as he did so. He found his way to the seat behind the desk and sat down. He then looked straight into the camera.

When his face became visible, Andrew jerked backward—despite the fact that the specter in front of him was actually thousands upon thousands of miles below him.

The flesh on the man's cheeks hung down in bloodied rags, and only the angle of the light protected Andrew from seeing the exposed jaws within them. Where his eyes should have been were ragged sockets, and red tears welled up out of them to course down what was left of his face. They spattered the surface of the desk.

"Can anyone see me?" he asked weakly. "Can anyone see me?"

His plaintive question was repeated for another hour, and if the delusional corpse expected an answer, Andrew had no idea where it would have come from.

After he finished addressing his lifeless audience, the man stepped away from the news desk and shuffled out of sight, making gurgling noises that could have been sobs.

Andrew spent another six hours watching the screen before he was satisfied that the channel, like all others, was dead.

Even with this knowledge, Andrew would come to the communications room every day for two weeks to sit and watch the computer track every available channel on every available spectrum for some change. There was none.

One week after their final orders from Houston had been given, the world below them was silent.

Barbara would come every so often and stand in the doorway to watch him watch the screens. She never interfered or even spoke, but let him keep his vigil.

He knew she was worried about him, worried about his obsession with monitoring the empty channels. Looking back, he was uncertain why each day of those two weeks would find him in the communications room. Perhaps he needed to be absolutely sure that the world he knew was gone before he could walk away from it.

She need not have worried. When the two weeks had passed, Andrew, now satisfied that it was all over, asked the computer to alert them of any new transmission, then left the room. He had not been back since.

The computer finished its calculations and flashed its findings on the screen.

Andrew was pacing the other side of the room. "Anything?"

Barbara read the screen and then read it again to be certain. "No, nothing." She sighed. "Why are we doing this, anyway?"

"You know why," he replied, his voice strained.

She stood up and walked to him. "Then tell me again, because I need to hear it again."

"We're it," he said. "There's no one else left who can. It's our responsibility to keep the human race going."

Barbara shook her head. "Do you know how insane that is? If we have a son, for example, who's he going to mate with? The computer? There's no nice girl down the street anymore, Andrew."

"*Andrew*," he thought and winced. *She only calls me Andrew when she's really upset.* "I know that, but—"

"But nothing," she interrupted, "what if we have two children, and they're both boys? That's not conducive to the propagation of a race, is it? And what if we do have a son and a daughter?"

"Incest—" he began.

"Is the least of our concerns," she cut him off again. "I'm talking about a highly restricted gene pool. We cannot, not the two of us, start the human race over again."

"That's how it started the first time, so they say." He winked in hopes to brighten her mood.

"Oh, spare me." She waved him away and then turned her back. Then after a moment, she added, "You don't have any apples in your garden anyway."

"I could try growing some, if it would make you feel better," he offered after a moment.

She faced him; she was trying not to smile. "Haven't you already tempted me enough as it stands?" she asked.

They crossed the room and embraced. "Barb, I'm sorry," he said into her shoulder.

"No, *I'm* sorry," she replied. "I just…it's not the same. Not here. I have to wonder what the point is sometimes."

"I do the same thing," he explained. "But the weight's on our shoulders, kiddo."

"I know," she told him. "I know. Children would be wonderful if we had a real world to raise them in, but all right." She turned her head a bit. "You know, I was the C.O. on this mission. I could order you to leave me alone."

"Would you shoot me for disobeying a direct order?"

She pretended to think about it for a moment. "No, I don't think so. It'd be even more boring without you around."

They held each other tightly, though Andrew could not take his eyes off the computer screen, with the word NEGATIVE seeming to stand out in letters larger than they actually were.

Two days after eight members of their ten person crew had left the station, and two days before a replacement team would have arrived, the screen in the communications room had sprung to life.

Barbara and Andrew heard the computer calling over the intercoms: incoming message from Houston.

On the screen was the face of their contact at ground control, Ed Klarner. He had dark circles under his eyes, and a beard was taking shape on the outskirts of his face. "Barbara, Andrew, hello," he said. "We don't have a lot of time, so let me get right to the point. You might have heard reports in the last few days of the new virus which sprang up in Africa."

"Yes," Barbara replied. "I thought they had the situation under control."

"They did," Ed told them, "but last night multiple cases appeared along the Eastern seaboard and no one knows how or why."

"Terrorists?" Andrew asked. Terrorists using biochemical warfare had always been a favorite phobia of his, ever since three years back when a nice gentleman from the Far East had been caught trying to put a mutated strain of cholera into the Manhattan water supply.

"No one knows," Ed replied. "It may be just a natural outbreak, we may never know. The incubation period is around three days, so people who think they're still healthy run from infested areas only to spread the virus wherever they go. Once the virus does take hold, it's usually fatal within twenty-four hours."

"Jesus," Barbara breathed.

"Well, some people are waiting for Him to show up any minute," Ed confided. "What I'm trying to say is it doesn't look good. Martial law has been declared east of the Mississippi River, but no one believes it's going to do any good. When the ebola virus hit Brazil a few years ago, you could wait it out because it would burn itself out quickly. This one," Ed paused. "This one seems to wait for you to spread it to someone else before it kills you. Hell, for all we know it's airborne. No one seems to be able to live long enough to draw any conclusions."

Neither Andrew nor Barbara knew what to say. They held hands without thinking, though it was not out of any emotion other than fear. It would be two months before Barbara would come to Andrew's room in the middle of the night and not sleep in her own again. At that point, watching Ed's face and hearing his words, they were simply two small children, clutching at each other, facing the unknown.

"What I'm trying to say is this," Ed wiped at his forehead with a handkerchief. "I know the company would shit if they knew I was being this frank with you, but they have bigger fish to fry now. You were there two weeks before any of this started up, so I think you're both fine. You've got everything you need to stay fine for a long, long time. But as for all of us down here...I think it's over, guys. I really do. I wish I had better news, but that's all the news I have to give you."

"Maybe they'll come up with something, Ed," Andrew offered. "You never know."

Ed shook his head, tears forming at the corners of his eyes. "Molly started coughing this morning and she can't seem to stop."

They both knew Molly Klarner. She had played hostess for the party that was thrown for them before they went up. She had smiled at them as she passed out finger foods.

"So I have to go home and see if I can't do something to help her. I just wanted the two of you to hear it from me so there would be no question. Your final orders are to keep living." He looked at them through the screen. "Do you understand?"

"Yes, sir," Barbara said. Andrew felt like he should say something as well but could not seem to speak.

"Very well," Ed stated, collecting himself. "This is Houston, signing off."

The screen went blank and stayed that way.

Barbara sat at the terminal, flipping through a digitized version of Albert Camus' collected works. *Until the world ended, I never had time to read all the masterpieces of literature*, she thought flippantly to herself.

The designers of their computer systems had wanted them to have as much information as possible, so that while even the vastness of the station would be too small for their physical frames, their minds could go wherever they wanted them to.

In the days immediately following the last transmission from Ed Klarner, she used several data cartridges for downloading libraries. She had had no idea how long the power would still be up on the world below, and it seemed important to her to keep alive whatever she could. The only evidence she had that some of the best libraries in the world had ever existed was now on digital media, under her care. *Preventing a global Alexandria*, she thought suddenly and winced.

She was certain some children's classics were on her cartridges, too. She sighed. Her mind always seemed to drift inevitably to the same subject. Despite this, the idea of bringing a child into the confinements of the station was anathema.

Not that she didn't want to have children; that was not the issue at all. She was thirty-four, and somewhere within her a clock was ticking. Under normal circumstances, she would have settled down with Drew and gotten about the business of having those children long ago. After all, even though medical science had raised the age women could expect to give birth to healthy children from forty to near fifty, the clock inside her did not give this credence. It continued to remind her that her days were passing her by.

These were not normal circumstances, as she had tried to explain to Drew. She also tried to explain it to herself, but despite all of this, she so wanted to have a child.

Perhaps it was the idea that someday, despite their perfectly enclosed environment where everything—including the food and power—was self-perpetuating, one of them would die. One of their bodies would simply wear out and quit, leaving the other completely alone.

What would that be like, she wondered, *to be the last person alive?* Not the last person on Earth, since there were none of those left and she and her mate were far above the surface of the planet... but the last person *anywhere?*

She shuddered at the thought. With Drew around, she was able to keep such dark thoughts at bay. But the idea of him being gone and her footfalls echoing through the station alone drove a portion of her mind toward panic.

Then once she had died, this station could just self-perpetuate until it finally fell out of the sky. Is that why they had been trying to conceive a child? For no other reason than a cure for loneliness? Was that a good enough reason?

It did not appear to matter, she mused. They could not seem to have a child—

She wanted to finish that thought with "to save our lives," a phrase she used often but found too apropos in this case.

What if I'm the problem? What if I'm barren? The idea swam in the depths of her mind often these days, but now it surfaced and presented itself. What if? That would be just perfect, wouldn't it? You have man and woman, the last pair, floating in an ark, and while the man is bursting at the seams with virility, the woman's womb is useless.

And that might be it, she thought. *One part of one woman's body that doesn't work and it's exit stage left for the human race. And no biological miracles here. Down on the surface, they had ways to get around a condition like I might have, but up here I have neither the tools nor the prowess.*

They had not considered this possibility, that she was the reason they could not get pregnant. She would need to get tested.

Andrew looked out the window at the dark clouds which hung over the western portion of what had been the United States. They had apparently spread into Washington State and Idaho. *I wonder how far it will go*, he thought, *with no one alive to stop it?*

Andrew had been quite the fan of science fiction as a boy growing up on the farms. His mind kept returning to an alien race, somewhere in the far flung future, arriving at the dead planet Earth. Almost nine billion archeological findings below, and two in orbit around the planet.

Death, he thought and wondered again whether he should try to garden up some form of alcohol. He had the ability to start a row of grapes, why not?

He shook his head. Drinking would not solve this problem.

Why was it so different now, he wondered. Why worry about the prospects of an ending now? He was thirty-two years old. The average life span of a human had reached ninety years. In the station, with its pristine environment, he might never get sick. He might live longer than that. Why be wracked with despair when you have another sixty years to look forward to? With a companion, no less.

Andrew turned away from the burning continent. Perhaps it was the idea that after the two of them died, it would be over. Maybe you could die at peace with the knowledge that someone would be around to bury you, or cremate you, or remember you, or…something. No human being would be there to mourn for him when he died except perhaps for Barbara.

Women live statistically longer than men, he reminded himself. *You may indeed be checking out first.*

It didn't even matter that Barbara was steadily turning the station into a time capsule of sorts, so that if some alien race did ever run across their remains, they would at least know that human culture, for a brief span, had been something.

Maybe that was why he wanted a child. Selfishly, he wanted someone to stand over his dead body and remember him. Didn't someone say once that the whole reason we have children is to achieve some kind of immortality?

"What an excuse," Andrew breathed. He looked around him at his hydroponic gardens. "One day, Andrew Jr., all of this will be yours." He laughed and fought back tears.

It didn't seem to matter anyway; they couldn't get pregnant. *Maybe that was a blessing*, he mused. Was he ready to deliver a child with the computer as midwife? Perhaps not. And despite Barbara's logic to answer the question of what they would do with the child once he (*or she*, he reminded himself) arrived, he feared that part of him was wistfully thinking of humans below the earth in airtight shelters, living and breathing and planning to retake the surface world.

Too much science fiction, he scolded himself. No one could have anticipated the end, if everything Ed had said was so. The world had ended within a week, and even if people had retreated to what they thought of as safety, three days later they would have started vomiting blood. No, there was no nice girl or boy living down the street, or even beneath the street in this case.

Still, it was a non-issue at present. Knowing that they were both the models of health, both from their entrance exams to the company and from follow-up tests administered by the computer, they had stopped using any kind of protection four months ago.

It had been a mutual decision. They had felt the weight upon them, this responsibility they had as caretakers to an entire species, and decided to try to do something about it.

Every week they would go and every week the computer would say NEGATIVE on its screen.

What if he was sterile?

This was an idea that had not occurred to him. All the checks the company had done on him had been for things which could have posed a problem to the mission—viable sperm count was never considered. *Wouldn't it be funny*, he asked himself, *if you were responsible for the demise of a species because you were shooting blanks?*

He decided a moment later, no, not really. He didn't think it would be funny at all.

He would need to be tested. Then he would at least know where they stood.

They sat next to each other, held hands and said nothing. They waited for the computer to finish its tests.

"At least we'll know," Barbara said, uncertain of who she was trying to comfort.

"I'm suddenly not sure I want to know," Andrew replied, gripping her hand.

She looked at him, a sudden fear taking her. "You...won't hate me if I—"

"Hate you?" He laughed. "How could I hate you? And I'm not just saying that because you're the last woman alive."

She laughed with him in spite of herself.

"No, I couldn't hate you. Not for this, not for anything." He thought for a moment. "Now, if you shorted out the gravity generators, then I might *dislike* you for a while…"

She was laughing harder. "You're making my stomach hurt."

"You—wouldn't hold it against me if I'm the problem, will you?" He asked, still wearing his smile.

She touched his cheek. "Of course not. But you know, there's this great male fertility clinic in Boston…"

"I bet if we called them we'd get their answering machine," He finished for her.

They both laughed again, hugging each other.

When the computer beeped, their humor came to an abrupt halt.

Andrew got up to look, but Barbara pushed him back down. She kissed him and then went to the computer screen. She had run the tests: her second was mission doctor, so it was her responsibility.

"Well, I guess that settles it," she said.

Andrew stood up and went to look. "Settles it? What is it?"

She turned to face him, blocking the screen. "I'm sorry, baby." She touched his face.

Oh God, it's me, he thought and his heart sank.

"We both struck out." She smiled weakly.

He looked at her. "What are you saying?"

"I'm saying that neither one of us is capable. I can't bear a child and even if I could, you couldn't impregnate me." She stepped aside. "See for yourself."

Andrew read the screen. "I don't know whether to be disappointed or relieved," he confessed.

"Then be both," Barbara told him. She was starting to cry. "Because I'm both."

He put his arms around her. "So I guess we're it," he said, tears forming in his eyes.

"We've got a long time being it though before we have to worry," she replied and kissed him.

"So what do we do now?"

"Follow orders and make the best of it, I suppose," she answered.

He laughed. "I guess you're right. Could take years, though."

Their relief broke from them in laughter as they clutched each other in the sparse sterility of the medical room.

Far below them and unnoticed, the fire spread eastward, driven on by wind, consuming and cleansing everything in its path.

The Day They Let Bernard Leave

"Honey. Honey, you need to get up," he heard his wife saying. He opened his eyes and immediately began to squint at the bedside table, searching for his glasses. They were placed in his hand. "Here you are, dear."

Bernard put them on and blinked as the world swam reluctantly into focus.

Jill was standing by the bed, already dressed. Bernard rubbed at his eyes for a moment, incredulous. Jill was never out of bed by the time he left for work, much less ready to go out. Instead of her customary robe and slippers, she was dressed in a suit he had not seen her wear since she was laid off two years back. Bernard blinked again for good measure, but the fact that his wife looked good remained. Just as a smile began to form on his face, he suddenly realized that if Jill was already dressed then it had to be almost noon. He had overslept, and was now extremely late for work. He jerked his head around to look at the clock on the bedside table.

"It's only six, Bernard, you're not late," she reassured him.

Bernard breathed a sigh of relief. Two years he had been working on a promotion. One day of waltzing in past nine o'clock and you could shove all of that out the window.

That worry discarded, he proceeded to smile at his wife. As his mind was drawn further out of sleep, he looked her up and down. He decided that given further, more conscious inspection, she looked better than good. She looked absolutely stunning.

"You look wonderful," he told her. "I always liked that outfit. Special occasion?" If there was one, he had no idea what it might be. He checked his internal calendar. Could he have missed her birthday? No, of course not. It was April, and Jill's birthday was in October.

Another thought struck him. *It's not* my *birthday, is it?* No, of course not. His birthday was in January.

"Yes, a very special occasion. Would you like some breakfast?" Jill asked cheerily. "I went out earlier this morning and bought all your favorites: wheat bread for toast with that blackberry jam, eggs, and some bacon."

For a moment, Bernard didn't know what to say. He could not believe what he was hearing. Jill hated to make breakfast; she had told him so on more than one occasion. While the office cafeteria had decent eggs, he had missed in vain the days when his wife used to cook for him. He offered once to make her breakfast instead, but she had simply stayed in bed until he left for work, rising only to get some coffee in preparation for the parade of talk shows and soap operas.

"Jill," he said finally, "I would love some breakfast, but...are you sure you would like to make breakfast?" He chose his words carefully, remembering one day, several months ago, when he had almost run late. He asked her to pour him a bowl of cereal. She had yelled and thrown a book at him. Based on this, he decided that he might need to be ready to dodge a projectile at any moment. Still, he reminded himself, she had made a trip to the supermarket for him.

She leaned forward and Bernard almost flinched. "Of course I would like to. It's a day unlike any other day. Anything you want, Bernard." She looked to the closet. "Go ahead and get dressed. I've already ironed your pants. Breakfast should be ready in about twenty minutes, so don't dally." She kissed him on his forehead and then walked out of the room.

Bernard watched his wife leave, and then shook his head. He put two fingers to the place on his forehead where she had kissed him. He pinched himself as well, but from what he could tell, he was already awake. *No, Bernard,* he assured himself, *this is actually happening.*

She had not kissed him in over a year, and that last one had been a cursory gesture at best. Any time he tried to make some kind of advance, no matter how small, she laughed or brushed it off as nothing. He sometimes wondered whether or not his wife was going through "The Change," whatever that meant. It was a term he had overheard one day on a television talk show. He kept meaning to go to the library and get some more information on it. It had not been a priority, though, for who wanted to suggest to their wife that she needed to see a doctor, when it would give her an excuse to throw a hairbrush at you?

He shaved and got dressed quickly, eager to go downstairs and receive further evidence that he was not hallucinating.

Jill was in the kitchen as promised, spooning some scrambled eggs onto a plate. "Your timing is perfect," she beamed, and motioned for Bernard to sit.

Bernard did as he was instructed. Jill placed his meal in front of him. He took several bites before the thought struck him: *I wonder if she's finally gone over the edge and decided to poison me?* He looked down at his bacon, two pieces of which he had already consumed. *Too late to worry about that now,* he decided and continued eating.

After another moment, he realized that Jill was not eating. Instead, she was standing, leaning on the back of another chair and watching him. "You won't join me?" he asked, feeling somewhat braver since they had managed to exchange words without a fight breaking out.

She shook her head. "No, dear, I'm not hungry right now. Just very excited." She pointed at his plate. "Is it good?"

Bernard smiled. "The best ever," he said.

"I'm glad." She continued to watch him.

Bernard munched on a piece of toast. "You said this was a special occasion," he prompted.

"Yes, I did. And yes, it is." She said no more.

Bernard took a sip of juice. "I see." He could not help but smile. "And...you're not going to tell me what it is."

The look on her face made it obvious that she would love to tell him. "Oh, Bernard, it's such wonderful news! I do wish I could tell you, but They've told me I can't."

Bernard stared at her. "They? They who?"

"You'll find out," Jill said, absolutely beside herself with not telling him. "Mr. Cummings is going to give you the news when you get to work. It's all decided."

Bernard nodded. "I see." In actuality, he did not see at all. He was extremely confused, but so as not to upset his wife, he nodded.

He finished his breakfast, looking uneasily at Jill the entire time. When he told her how much he enjoyed and appreciated the meal, she tried to tear his head from his shoulders with an affectionate yet excruciating bear hug.

"I've already got your briefcase by the front door, and if you leave now, you can be at the bus stop in time for the next run." She escorted him to the foyer and then stopped, turning to face him. "Bernard, there's something I need to say." She cleared her throat and seemed to be searching for the right way to express herself. "I know that our marriage hasn't been the easiest thing in the world, and that I haven't been the easiest person in the world to get along with—"

Bernard tried to step in, thinking he was hearing a cue for him to do so. "Jill, honey—"

She shushed him. "No, Bernard, it's true and we both know it, so just let me finish. We've both had our shortcomings, but I think we did okay for ourselves, all things considered. And I hope you agree." Before he could respond, she continued, "So when you finally do meet Them, be sure to tell Them about me. Don't forget me, is what I'm trying to say." Unbelievably, a tear formed at the corner of her left eye.

Bernard wiped the tear away, touched. Truly, he had no idea what was transpiring here. Another mention of "Them," whoever in the world "They" might be. And now his wife was talking as though she would never see him again. If the breakfast had been poisoned, he decided now the poison was a slow-acting one. He had to get out of the house, go to work, and simply hope that Mr. Cummings would have some answers for him. For all he knew, this was some vast joke that the guys at work had decided to play on him. Granted, his co-workers were the most humorless men that Bernard had ever had the disservice to work with, but at present it was the most plausible theory he could muster.

"Sweetheart," he finally decided to say, "how could I forget you?"

Jill embraced him violently again. "That's the nicest thing anyone has ever said to me," she cried.

Bernard could not help but think, *'I do' isn't in the running?*

Jill released him and held him at armslength. She was crying in earnest. "Now go. Go, before you miss your bus."

Definitely a chemical imbalance of some sort, Bernard decided firmly. He made a mental note to stop by the library after work and get some more information.

He walked out the front door, stopping midway to the sidewalk to wave at his wife, who was dabbing at her face with a tissue. He rounded the corner and went to the bus stop.

He sat down on the bench, shaking his head. *What an extraordinarily strange day*, he thought.

Two minutes passed, and the bus pulled up. The doors swung open with a swish.

Bernard stepped on and fished in his pocket for some coins.

The driver looked at him, perplexed. He squinted at Bernard and then opened his eyes wide. "Hey, buddy," the driver said, "it's okay. Today it's on the house."

Bernard looked at the driver as though he had gone mad. This was the same driver who would throw you bodily from the vehicle if you asked for change. The throwing would take place while the bus was moving if you had anything larger than a one dollar bill.

"Come on," the driver offered amicably. "My gift to you."

Bernard nodded again, placating another madperson. He gave the driver as wide a berth as he could given the enclosed space. When he was satisfied that he was out of grabbing and throwing range, and that the driver was now piloting the bus and thus too busy to assault him, he turned to make his way down the aisle and find a seat.

The entire population of the bus was staring at him intently.

A young woman at the front stood up. "Here, sir, you can have my seat."

Bernard was about to tell her that it was perfectly all right, but she was gone, practically sprinting down the aisle. He said thank you and sat down.

Everyone on the bus still watched him, as though waiting to see what his next move would be.

The young man to his right cleared his throat, preparing to speak.

Bernard sat and braced himself for whatever might come next.

"Are you...Bernard Robertson?" The boy asked tentatively.

Bernard was beginning to wonder about the answer to that question himself. He went with the only answer he knew. "Yes."

The boy's face brightened and a collective sigh shimmered throughout the bus. "I thought so," he beamed. "May I shake your hand?"

Bernard's eyebrows went up. *This certainly is an elaborate joke*, he thought. "I don't see why not," he told the young man, offering his hand.

The young man shook it earnestly. "It's a pleasure to meet you, sir."

"Thank you," Bernard said, his head ringing.

The bus went eerily silent, and Bernard was glad the ride was only ten minutes long. That time was spent looking out the window and trying to pretend that everyone on the bus was not watching him look out the window.

Bernard found himself wondering whether or not the change he suspected Jill was undergoing was somehow communicable.

Finally, the bus crawled to a stop. Bernard shot up, ready to get out as soon as possible, find Mr. Cummings and get some answers.

The girl who had given him her seat stood up in back. "Good luck, sir," she called out, and was greeted with a chorus of agreement from the rest of the passengers.

"Thank you," Bernard offered weakly as he stumbled onto the sidewalk. The bus drove off, everyone on board waving at him as it went.

Bernard pondered a new possibility: perhaps he had hit his head on something and, unbeknownst to himself, was lying in a hospital bed in a coma, dreaming this entire day. At this point, it seemed to be the only explanation which could account for everything he had so far experienced. Because of this, he kept it waiting in the wings just in case he needed it.

He was glad he met with little notice on his way into the building and during the elevator ride. However, what he did receive was more than enough. No one stopped to try and shake his hand, but everywhere people would stop and stare and whisper to one another in his wake.

Bernard opened the door to his company's office and stepped in. The receptionist, a young brunette named Sandy, popped up from behind her desk as if somewhere a button had been pressed. She smiled. "Mr. Robertson, I—"

He stalked toward her desk. "Sandy, stop right there," he commanded. "Now, tell me—why do you look so happy to see me? Why is everyone so amazed and happy to see me? Most days you don't even look up when I walk into this office. Now you've got to tell me: just what in God's name is going on?"

Her smile broadened. "Mr. Robertson, I know you're confused. That's understandable. But Mr. Cummings is expecting you. They've asked him to explain everything to you."

"'They'? Who are 'They'?"

Sandy fingered his necktie and dropped her voice. "Listen. Mr. Cummings probably isn't expecting you for another ten minutes or so. You're actually early. What say we pop into one of the meeting rooms for a second or two? I've never made it with a guy who was—"

A door swung open to their right. Mr. Cummings stepped out. "Sandy, has—" he began, and then his eyes found Bernard, who was being pulled by his tie toward the waiting lips of the receptionist. "Bernie!" he called out, taking large strides into the room.

Bernard wondered at this. *He never calls me 'Bernie.'*

Mr. Cummings gave Bernard a hearty handshake and rescued him from Sandy's clutches. She blew a kiss as he was being led away. "Sandy, hold my calls," Mr. Cummings declared over his shoulder.

His office door swung shut.

For some reason, Bernard thought that Mr. Cummings looked nervous. "Have a seat, Bernie. Have a seat." He gestured to one of the large plush chairs in front of his desk, and Bernard did as he was instructed.

Mr. Cummings sat for a moment, unsure of himself. He fidgeted with his tie. Finally, he looked up at Bernard and a grin spread across his face. "Would you like anything? Coffee? Something?"

"No, sir."

Mr. Cummings' face became very serious. "Of course. You want to get to the bottom of what's been happening today."

Bernard leaned forward in his chair. "So you *do* know—"

"Yes, Bernie, I do. It must have been pretty strange, not knowing why things are the way they are, right?"

Bernard nodded frantically. "Yes, sir. My wife, and then everyone on the bus…" He didn't know whether he should mention that

Sandy had propositioned him in the foyer of the office, so he left that part out.

"I understand. I've never seen this type of thing happen before, to be perfectly honest. I mean, I heard about it once, but you never believe that this type of thing goes on. I mean, it happens so infrequently..."

Bernard felt the shred of hope, that someone was for once going to give him a straight answer, fray out of existence. "I'm afraid I don't quite follow you, Mr. Cummings."

One of Mr. Cummings' hands went to his face; a finger tapped at his lips impatiently. His thoughts were momentarily heavy. "Hmmm," he finally sighed. "No, Bernie, I'm afraid I don't make much sense talking about it. Maybe I wasn't the best choice to tell you. But, well, you know: They're always right!"

Bernard pointed at Mr. Cummings. "See, that's the part where I lose it completely. Who are 'They'? No matter who I talk to today, they're always referring to 'They,' and no one will give me a straight answer."

"I guess the main thing you need to know," Mr. Cummings continued, streaming past his employee's concern, "and what I've been supposed to tell you—and doing a poor job of it, I might add—is that you're free to go." He held out his hands and smiled. "You're free to go." He said this as if he were delivering a benediction to a sizable congregation.

Bernard's jaw did more than drop at that moment; it tried to separate itself from the rest of his skull. "I'm— I'm—" He tried desperately to find enough air in his lungs to express himself. "—fired?" He finally croaked the last word out.

Mr. Cummings' face went pale. "No! Oh, no, no, my dear boy. Bernie, no." He reached across his desk, took Bernard's hand and patted it. "No, forgive me. That's not it at all. Not it at all."

After a minute or so of Mr. Cummings' frantic apologies, Bernard remembered how to breathe again.

"I'm so sorry, Bernie, it's nothing like that at all."

Bernard straightened up in his chair. "So what is it, then? 'Free to go.' I don't understand."

"Let me put it to you as plainly as I possibly can," Mr. Cummings prefaced.

Bernard leaned forward. This was the best proposition he had heard all day, even including Sandy's.

"You've been granted a very special privilege. An honor, if you will. That's why everyone has been treating you strangely."

A promotion? Bernard's mind anticipated. *A raise? What?*

"They've told us that you're free to leave. The experiment. Your part of the experiment is over, and you can go."

Bernard's head reeled. He knew from experience that no one would answer him if he asked who "They" were, so he tried a different approach instead. "What experiment? Mr. Cummings, I'm afraid I don't understand."

"It's quite all right, Bernie," Mr. Cummings reached for the intercom. "I think the best thing is to let Them explain it Themselves."

Bernard thought that sounded reasonable enough.

Mr. Cummings pressed the intercom button. "Sandy, please ask the gentlemen to come in."

Within moments, two burly "gentlemen" were squeezed into the office as well.

Bernard eyed the two men in their white uniforms warily. "These are 'Them'?" he asked Mr. Cummings uneasily.

"No, no, my boy," Mr. Cummings shook his head. "They're going to take you to Them."

At this, the two large men each clamped down on one of Bernard's arms. "Hey!" Bernard cried out. "What are you doing?"

They began to drag him out of the office, oblivious to his protestations. He saw Sandy stand up at her desk. "I offered, but you missed out," she said sadly. "Just remember me when you see Them, huh?"

Bernard jerked his head around and saw Mr. Cummings standing in his office doorway. "Just relax, it's a great honor that's about to be bestowed upon you." He waved. "Good luck, son. Remember me when you meet Them. Remember how I always tried to be good to you."

With that, the two men had carried him around a corner and down a long hallway. "Where are you taking me?" he asked them.

Neither answered. Neither even looked at him; they kept their eyes focused straight ahead. Bernard finally quit looking up at them and followed their gaze.

At the end of the hallway that held entrances to all the various conference rooms, there was a door marked "Janitor." That seemed to be their destination.

Bernard's mind, weakened by the morning, thought madly, *That's my honor? 'They' are going to make me a janitor?*

Within seconds, they had reached the closet at the end of the hall. One of Bernard's escorts stuck out a meaty hand and turned the knob. The door swung open to reveal white. There was nothing but white as far as the eye could see.

Bernard tried to bring up a hand to shield himself from the glare, but seconds later determined that there was no glare to shield his eyes from.

The two men pushed him through the door and then shut it behind him before he could protest.

When he turned to bang on the door to demand he be let out, he had the stunned realization that the outline of the door was no longer visible. In fact, there was no evidence he had just passed through a portal at all. He took three steps forward, past where he was sure the door should be, and encountered no obstacle. Instead he saw only the white stretching out in all directions, with no real distinction between floor and ceiling, or ground and sky. There was nothing else.

"Don't wander far," a voice behind him cautioned. "I wouldn't, anyway."

Bernard turned around.

Sitting on a bench which he had not noticed before in his mad rush to return to wherever it was he had come from was a man in a suit. He was leaning forward over his knees, with his hands between them, fidgeting aimlessly with the necktie he was no longer wearing. He looked over at Bernard with passing interest.

"I'm sorry," Bernard said, walking toward the man. "What did you say?"

"I said, don't wander far. Those that do don't seem to ever come back." He looked out into the white void. "I think they get turned around out there and wander around for...I don't know. Eternity. Something like that."

Bernard came over and sat down next to the man. "I'm Bernard Robertson." He extended a hand.

The man stared at the hand for a moment, perplexed, his eyes searching it. Then, a thought crossed him. "Oh, a handshake. I'm sorry." The man took Bernard's hand and shook it in earnest. "It's been a long time," he laughed. "Hang on." He fished in his coat pocket and produced his wallet. He flipped through it until he came to his driver's license. "Frank," he addressed himself. "Yes, that's right. Frank McDonald. That's me. Pleased to meet you, Bernard."

Bernard stared dumbfounded as the man put his wallet away. "You *have* been here a long time, haven't you, Frank?"

Frank nodded. "I think so. Feels like it. Can't be sure. Watch broke a long time ago."

Bernard looked down at his own watch. The LED read all zeros.

"Are we the only people here?" Bernard asked.

"Hard to say," Frank confided. "There were a couple of people here when I arrived, but they got sick of waiting, so they picked a direction and started walking. Never saw them again."

"Why didn't you go?"

"What's the point? Look out there," Frank pointed into the seeming distance. "It's all the same as it is here. Except for this bench. At least here you can sit. What's the point?" He shrugged.

Bernard let a few moments pass, trying to let his thoughts coagulate into another question. "So, what are we waiting for?"

Frank looked at him. "Didn't they tell you? We're waiting for Them. They'll explain everything."

"What do you mean by 'everything'?"

"I mean why we're here. Why we were *there*," Frank gestured at the space where the door of a janitor's closet had been just minutes before. "They'll explain everything."

Another few moments of silence passed. "Do you believe it?" Bernard asked him.

Frank frowned. "Of course I believe it. What else is there?" He sat back and relaxed. "You don't have a smoke on you, do you?"

Bernard shook his head no.

"Don't smoke, huh? Smart man." Frank sighed. "I've been trying to quit. Still, it'd be nice if They brought some smokes with Them."

Bernard considered asking Frank who "They" were, but instead found himself wondering what difference it made. He leaned back on the bench and tried his best to get comfortable.

Adelaide

The door to the apartment opened slowly and the old man stepped in. He turned around to secure the locks with hands that obeyed one command in three. Two paces into the living room and there was the cat, sitting on the floor and looking expectantly up at him.

They spent a moment simply staring at each other. Then the old man held up a finger, as if asking the cat to wait for a moment. He went into the kitchen. From within came the sound of a glass being filled from a tap, followed by a brief struggle with what might have been the childproof top to a medicine bottle. A minute or so later, the old man stepped back into the living room, drinking the last of the water. He held the glass in minutely trembling hands, using both to ensure it would not go shattering to the floor.

The cat remained patiently where it was, simply turning its head to watch the man's progress.

The old man held up a finger again, as if he had just remembered something. He looked as if he might have snapped his gnarled and arthritic fingers, but the days when that was an option were long gone. He disappeared into the kitchen once more, and there was a sound of more running water. After this, an electric can opener was heard three times in succession.

The old man came out of the kitchen for the last time, seemingly contented. His glass of water was full again, and he set it on the TV tray next to his chair.

Once the old man had settled in, the cat broke its pose to come and sprawl itself across his lap. This pleased him, for he stroked the cat's fur with one hand while he studied the medicine bottle he had brought from the kitchen.

"Take one pill before going to sleep." He sighed and tossed the bottle to the floor, where it rolled emptily away. The cat paid it no mind. It seemed to study the old man's face, as if looking for answers.

"I'm dead," he croaked happily. "Bone cancer."

The tail swished distractedly across his thigh as the cat turned its head away.

"It's never been a pretty business, death—has it?" the old man asked. "It's always ugly, it's just a matter of degrees of ugliness.

"You don't begrudge me it, do you?" he asked, scratching the cat's ears.

The cat's only reply was to rub its head against the man's hand.

"I hope not. I pray that you don't," he sighed. "Larry, my brother—you remember. He had so many tubes running in and out of him, he didn't look like Larry anymore."

The old man gave out an involuntary shudder. "Took a month. We should count ourselves as among the lucky that it only took a month, long as it was, yes. A month of breathing with the help of a machine." He shook his head and took a sip of water. "That's no way for a man to go out."

The cat stared up at the man and blinked.

"Or a woman, either," he added. "Anyone. There's got to be some dignity in it somewhere. No matter how good the story is, if it doesn't end where and how it's supposed to, it loses its meaning."

The cat yawned.

The old man laughed, a sound high and cracking. "You always were a tough audience. I guess that's part of the reason you're here, isn't it? I mean, you're right. An old man committing suicide in a broken down apartment has no more insight into the mind of God than the next man." He glanced at the cat, which looked indifferently up at him. "Or person," he added. "Maybe what's supposed to happen, happens. Maybe it does all the time and we never realize it.

"I don't know," he said simply, with a movement that could have been a shrug. "I thought about majoring in philosophy but I couldn't pass the key courses." He stroked the cat's fur. "You, on the other hand, had to tutor me, otherwise we wouldn't be here."

He stared out the window. "So many things seem to hinge on other things without which the first group of things would not have occurred. Hmmm," he trailed off.

For a moment, the man's eyes glazed over as he seemed to concentrate on some spot far in the distance.

The cat dug its claws slowly into the man's thigh.

He broke from his reverie. "Oh! No, not gone yet. Not yet." He rubbed the cat's neck. "You know, when it comes to death and its ugliness, I think you had the prettiest death possible." The creases on the old man's face deepened. "I woke up and you...didn't. In your sleep, you just...stopped. That was three years ago."

He stopped stroking the cat, and it lay across his legs, motionless.

"The first six months I wandered around in a daze. It felt like I had lost a part of my own body, and on certain days I could still feel that missing part. I could still feel you." He wiped a stray tear from his eye. "It was hard, Addy, so hard."

His hand began petting the cat again.

"Then, six months after that, you showed up on my doorstep. Literally. I didn't know what to think at first. I had always liked dogs, myself.

"But when I opened the door that day, you walked in like you owned the place. You came right over here to your favorite chair and curled up in it like it was where you belonged.

"It wasn't that that made me figure out it was really you. It wasn't the fact that you slept on your bed at night, either. It was the way you felt."

The cat looked up at him.

"Not physically," he explained. "Not that way at all. You just feel like you. How I'd know what room you were in when I came home from the store or how I would know to look up when you were watching me on the street from the window here. Like it was when you were alive.

"Then I had to wonder why you came back." The man took another sip of water. "It didn't take long to figure out. Of course, there's no way to prove my theory since you can't come right out and tell me. The reason I've come up with was that you, wherever you were, saw just how empty my life was without you in it, and you wanted to come back and keep me company." He peered down at the cat. "Maybe you missed me a little, too."

The cat yawned.

"Fine," he grunted. "Always a wise one, even after death. I should have known not even that would have cured you." He chuckled. "Came back to help keep me straight. And to help me deal with this."

He began petting the cat again. It lowered its head and purred softly.

"It didn't really throw me that you came back, Addy." He scratched his head and squinted out the window. "I never have thought of it before, how amazingly unbothered I was about the whole thing. I mean, if someone would have told me five years ago, 'Your wife's going to die in her sleep and come back a year later as a cat,' I'd have laughed that someone out of the building."

The cat rolled over on its side to give the old man access to its belly.

"No, I accepted it pretty much the day I had figured it out. But eventually, the question formed in my head: 'Why a cat?'"

The cat opened its eyes.

"Nothing wrong with cats. You never seemed to have a great fancy for cats while you were alive." He rubbed his forehead. "Never mentioned it if you did. We never had pets around. I'da figured if you had wanted a cat around the place, we were married for fifty-three years, you had plenty of time to tell me.

"But then, it hit me." The old man looked down at the cat. "You don't need anyone to take care of you. If I didn't feed you, you'd go out and hunt for something yourself. Water, same thing. Shelter—none of it needs to be given to you. Cats decide their masters—owners, whatever you want to call them—not the other way around. They can be pampered or they can fend for themselves out in the world. It's their choice. It's almost like...an extended vacation for a soul."

The cat switched sides so that the old man could distribute his attention evenly.

"You could be working very hard for all I know," he confessed. "You're almost as hard to read now as you were when you were a woman."

The cat nipped at the old man's finger. He drew it back in surprise, a small welt of blood standing out from the tip. "Although you can still express yourself quite well." He chuckled softly, sticking his finger in his mouth to suck on it for a moment.

He popped his finger out of his mouth. "I started to think about it. Really think about it, you know? We lived a long time, we saw a lot of things. Some of them were very strange. A couple of things I saw during the war were so strange I couldn't share them with you, the one person I shared everything with." He closed his eyes. "Now that you're dead, you probably know all about them and know why I never troubled you with them. I hope you understand." He shook his head, sadly. "It's bad enough that one of us had to have those things running around their head. No sense in both of us having to carry that burden.

"Still, it didn't seem so crazy. It's no crazier than anything else in this crazy world, anyway." He inspected his injured finger. "Maybe it's not just you, either. Maybe cats are people's spirits—souls, whatever—sent back to do whatever they see fit. Maybe you can earn the right to do that." He laughed. "Maybe—maybe people are reincarnated cats. Who knows?"

He shook his head again and looked down at the cat. Its eyes were closed, but the old man could tell by the cat's ears it was listening and not asleep.

"I don't really know if I buy all of that or any of it. I don't know if cats are here to help us or if I'm just a lonely old man dying of bone cancer and sleeping pills in his apartment and going insane the whole way down the hill." He lifted the cat in his arms. "Could be you are just a cat, a cat that an old man named Adelaide simply because he missed his dead wife." The old man stood up. "Could be, indeed."

He set the cat down on the chair. "I'm starting to feel it, Addy. I think I should go lay down before I fall down." He nodded his head, his eyes already dreaming. "I think that is a good idea."

He shuffled a few steps toward his bedroom door. "I put out a big bowl of water and three cans of food for you, just in case you would like to stay here for a while before you leave." He glanced up at the door. "Oh, yes," he said, and walked over. He worked the locks much easier this time and opened the door a couple of inches. He turned to the cat. "That way, you can leave when you think it's time."

He kneeled down slowly and carefully. The cat walked over to him. He put out a hand and the cat brushed its face against it. "Maybe they'll let me come back as a cat, too," he sighed. "Maybe you could put in a good word for me so they don't hold this against me. I'll try, just keep a watch for me. If I get back here, I'll find you." He smiled and stood up, one of his knees firing off a pistol shot.

"I need to sleep now," he said over his shoulder, stepping into the shadows of the bedroom. His footsteps shuffled across the floor and a moment later, there was the groaning of old springs as he laid down.

The cat watched the bedroom door for a moment before going inside.

An hour passed before the cat emerged again. She looked about the apartment slowly and then turned and left without bothering to close the door behind her.

Voodoo ver. 1.0

Simon Carlson looked out through his dirty windshield and sighed. Before him was the campus of Morrison School, a place that he had hoped he would never see again. It stood empty in the Saturday afternoon sun. The reason for Simon's visit, why he had braved this place again, was leaning in the front door and smiling.

Simon sighed once more for good measure and got out of the car. He had parked in the space that was marked H. EDGARS, PRINCIPAL in letters of yellow stencil, and this had given him some strange kind of satisfaction. "Hi, Ellen," he called across the parking lot.

His sister waved to him.

He walked around to the car's passenger side, opened the door and pulled out his laptop case.

Over the course of twelve years he had spent many a school day morning trudging this same route up to the same big green double doors. It was in this place he had learned the fine art of taping his glasses back together after their weekly trouncing by an upper classman. Back then, he would never have dreamed of someday playing the part of the good alumnus and doing something to aid his alma mater. The idea that his older sister would grow up to be a teacher at this school was entirely beyond the pale.

He finished the unpleasantly familiar walk and promptly received a hug. "Hi, Simon," Ellen said.

"Kids giving you fits?" he asked, as she held the door open for him.

She took his arm and escorted him down the hall. "Yeah, you could say that. I'm really glad you're here, Simon. You know they know more about this computer stuff than I do."

"They've been downloading games to the computers, huh?"

They turned to their right, into a hall lined with yellow lockers. One locker at the very end of the hall stood ajar, a textbook lying face down in front of it. Their footfalls careened off the walls and back at them.

Ellen rolled her eyes. "I'm not out the door for two minutes before they've got Space Control up and running."

"I think the game's called Space Command," Simon corrected. "Why don't you just delete them off the hard drive?"

"Believe me, I would if I could, but when I go to delete the game, I can't find it on the computer anywhere. It's disrupting my classes and making me crazy.

"And on top of all that: there's some bug going around the school. The principal's out sick, the vice principal has been here but on some antibiotics. I've got this crick in my neck that I can't seem to shake. We've been kind of just limping along the past couple of days."

"Well, I'll keep my distance," Simon smirked and took a step away from his sister. "After all, I—"

"—don't have time to be sick," Ellen finished for him. "Still Mister Impervious, huh? Well, you probably won't catch the crick in my neck, but I'll try not to cough on you or anything just to be safe."

They came to the computer lab. Above the door, "Ms. Ellen Carlson" was written in blue magic marker letters on a slab of off-green posterboard.

"In all of that complaining, did I manage to mention how grateful I am that you're here?" She asked, opening the classroom door.

"I figured it was in there someplace," Simon smiled and stepped in. He set his laptop case down on his sister's desk and then looked around at the twenty or so computers.

"So they're hiding the games on the hard drive, huh?" Simon

asked no one in particular. He came to the first system and powered on the machine. "Well, let's see how good they are." When the machine booted to a command prompt, Simon brought up a list of directories. "Ah," he pointed at the screen. There was a directory named SCONTROL. "There's your Space Control."

"I thought it was Space Command."

"Whatever," Simon deleted the directory. He went on to find two other games and delete them as well.

"I don't get it," Ellen said. "Where do they get the money to buy all of these games?"

"It's like this," he replied, stumbling over a directory called RACE500. "They don't buy them. They download them from the Internet or from electronic bulletin boards. They're called 'shareware,' which means you get a taste of the game, and if you like it and want the whole thing, you send someone money. Or you just download a hacked version of the game and play it for free anyway.

"See," he remarked, powering off machine number one, and moving on to the second, "if they were really good, they'd be hiding the directories."

Two minutes later, Simon grunted in satisfaction. "Okay, so they're hiding the directories." He had found a STARBASE directory that did not show up on a normal directory listing. He deleted it. "Yeah, yeah, but if they were really good, they'd put the directory in another directory, and then hide it. That's what I would do."

Three minutes later, Simon raised his eyebrows. "Okay, so they're good. Pretty good. They stuck this Kommander Krom game in the word processor's directory, interspersed with everything else, and then hid it." He looked up from the keyboard. "How old are these kids?"

"Ten through fourteen, for the most part. The high schoolers have their own computer lab on the west wing, and the elementary schoolers have their own in the south wing."

"Ten years old? I'm impressed," Simon remarked as he wiped out another SCONTROL directory. "I don't know if I could have figured this out at ten."

"Simon, when you were ten, you were still working on an abacus."

Simon shot a look at his sister. "Just remember, El, you're older than me."

"I'm sure if I ever do forget, you'll remind me. How's work been going?"

"Slow," Simon grunted. *Nonexistent*, he added silently to himself. Carlson Software, the company that was essentially Simon in his cramped bedroom-turned-office, was on the verge of becoming a nonentity. The support position that Simon had abandoned at a larger corporation was looking better all the time. He missed the elusive animal that seemed these days to only exist in those multinational companies: the steady paycheck. "It's all right, though," he lied nonchalantly.

Ellen stood in silence and watched her brother work for a few moments more, occasionally rubbing the back of her neck. Finally she asked, "You want a cola or something?"

Simon paused and considered. "Yeah, that'd be great." He began digging through his front pocket.

"My treat." She walked toward the door of the classroom.

"Did you need this done in the other two labs?"

She stopped. "Oh, no. That's Brenda and Josie's responsibility. They can get *their* little brothers out here if they need help." She grinned and walked out.

"Yadda yadda yadda," he mumbled loudly enough for her to overhear and moved down to the third system. Here again, he found SCONTROL and RACE500 and deleted them both. He figured he might be here for the better part of an hour, just finding games and erasing them. *Tell Brenda and Josie my rates are cheap*, he felt like calling after her, but he was not that desperate. Not yet, at least.

One thing Simon had neglected to mention to his sister was that he thought her predicament was quite humorous. A bunch of kids loading games on the systems they were supposed to be using for education—it sounded like something he would have done during his stay in this correctional facility.

He had almost become satisfied that the third system was clean when he found an additional subdirectory in one of the main directories, hidden like the others. VOODOO was its name.

Voodoo? Simon thought. *Voodoo? Race cars and battling aliens I can understand, but voodoo?*

Curious, he went into the VOODOO directory, typed in VOODOO and hit enter.

VOODOO, the screen said. *Version 1.0 (Unregistered version)*

If you use Voodoo for more than 15 days, please send $15 (in US funds) to...
Darren Curtis, P.O. Box 1536, Groverton MO 64112
http://houngansoftware.com
Click here twice to continue...

Simon studied the screen for a moment, before deciding it was probably just some game where you wandered around, blowing away zombies with a shotgun or some such nonsense. They created them all the time for the big gaming platforms, so perhaps this was just a knock off of that.

He clicked twice and the screen changed. On the screen was a toolbar, with most of the buttons greyed out. There was a pull-down menu bar, with two selections, *File* and *Help*. Simon clicked on *File*. Below the word *File*, Simon saw he now had a choice between *New Doll* and *Open*.

"'New Doll?'" Simon breathed. "What the hell *is* this?"

He clicked on *Open*, and a selection window appeared in the middle of the screen. In the VOODOO directory, there was a number of file choices: EDGARS.VOO, FAIRMONT.VOO, and HICKS.VOO. The first file on the list was CARLSON.VOO.

He spent a moment studying the screen, dumbfounded by what he was seeing. He clicked on CARLSON.VOO and the screen changed again. This time all the buttons on the toolbar became available. There was a button with what looked like a match on it, another with an ice cube, yet another with a knife. The first one on the toolbar was a pin, and the only reason he was certain of this was because of the image that appeared beneath the toolbar.

It was a doll, three-dimensionally rendered. It looked like one of those wooden dolls artists used in figure drawing, which you could pose in many different arrangements. In the doll's neck was a straight pin. To the right of the doll was a digitized picture of Ellen's face.

"What the hell—?" Simon asked out loud again.

He clicked on the match. A message appeared.

Sorry. Fire not available in the unregistered version.
Pins are the only accessory available in the unregistered version.
Register today!

Below it was the contact information again for where to send your fifteen dollars. He thought about clicking on an icon with what looked to be a bludgeon of some sort, but he didn't want to test its availability.

Simon felt as though a cinderblock had dropped into his stomach. He thought of the space where his car was parked and became suddenly quite sure why it had been available for the past couple of days.

Simon clicked on the straight pin in the doll's neck. A box appeared around it. He clicked again and a small menu appeared. His choices were *Copy*, *Delete* and *Deeper*. He clicked on *Delete* and the pin disappeared from the screen.

"Here's your cola, Simon," a voice said from the door.

Simon cried out. One hand went to his chest and the other to the table to steady himself. "Jesus, Ellen," he moaned.

Ellen looked shocked. In her hands were two canned soft drinks. "Sorry," she offered weakly. "Didn't know you were in another world."

Simon quickly saved his sister's doll, exited the game, if that was indeed what it was, and arrived back at a command prompt. He turned and accepted the drink, quickly popping the top and knocking back half the cola in one draught.

"Thirsty, huh?" Ellen looked at him closely. "Are you all right, Simon? You look pale."

"Fine," Simon replied. "Dandy. Peachy." He waited a beat. "How are *you*, El? How's your neck?"

Ellen ran a hand along the back of her neck. "You know, come to think of it, it feels a lot better."

Simon blinked. "What, did you take something?"

"No, I left my bottle of aspirin at home. Might take a couple when I get home anyway just in case it comes back." She plopped down in a chair next to him. "So, what am I going to do, call you in every month to get rid of my game infestation?"

Simon honestly had not considered that possibility. "I can write you up a simple set of instructions for going out and finding them, even if they're hidden."

She went up to her desk and produced a tablet from the top drawer. "Well, start dictating, and I'll jot them down as you go."

Simon spent his time on the next system explaining to his sister how to work the various commands he was using on his search and destroy mission. All the while, he would find himself glancing at the third machine, the one with the unique directory.

Forty-five minutes later, all the machines had received his clean bill of health and Ellen felt better knowing that she could continue after that point.

Ellen began powering the computers off on the far side of the room, and Simon went to do the same to the first table of computers. First, however, he went to his laptop case and pulled out a blank diskette. He stepped to the third machine and did a quick check of the VOODOO directory. *Jesus, the whole thing can fit on one diskette!* he thought to himself as he slipped the diskette into the drive and dumped the contents of the directory onto it.

When he was satisfied he had captured the entire directory, he deleted it from the machine and powered off all the machines on his side of the room.

"Say hey, little brother," Ellen walked over to him and put an arm around his shoulder. "What say I take you out for pizza? Your standard fee for freelance work, right?"

"That's a great idea," Simon began, "and any other time I'd say yes, but I've got a project back at the apartment that has to be done before Monday, and I'm a little behind."

"Why didn't you tell me? We could have done this another weekend—?"

Simon stopped her. "No, this didn't take long at all, and I needed a break. Still, El, thanks for the offer."

Ellen studied him for a moment. "All right, Simon, if you say so."

Back at the parking lot, she hugged and thanked him again. "Are you sure you're all right?" she asked him as he was climbing into his car.

"Fine, fine," he waved it off, "just got a lot of work to do. I'll check back and see how the rugrats are doing."

"Okay, take care," she said. Simon watched her wave to him from his rear view mirror.

Simon sat in his apartment, flipping the diskette around with his fingers. VOODOO, he had written on the label in large, black letters. He had drawn a skull and crossbones over that. *Ha ha*, he thought absently.

The files had tested fine when he ran them through his virus scanner. It was just a few data files and an executable. It was all on this diskette. It was just a lousy piece of shareware that someone had dreamed up as a joke...

"...and I don't get it," he declared softly to his empty apartment, "and worse, I'm afraid to load the damn thing."

Simon threw the diskette down on his desk and walked into the kitchen, yawning and ruffling his hair. A quick look at the clock on the stove showed it to be just after one o'clock in the morning.

If you're going to load the thing, do it and get it over with so we can go to sleep, a part of his mind cried out even as his hands poured another cup of coffee. He took a long sip and sat down at the kitchen bar.

"Darren Curtis..." he mumbled. "What the hell did you do? A virtual voodoo doll maker? That's insane."

Simon had gone through all the files on the diskette, trying to see how it was possible, but could find nothing out of the ordinary with the Voodoo program. It looked like a simple piece of shareware, written as a joke.

But he had seen it work! He deleted the pin from the neck of his sister's doll and miraculously she began feeling better.

So some kid had downloaded Voodoo and used it to make the principal and vice principal sick, and give his sister neck pains? Some ten-, eleven-year-old kid?

He walked back into his study and looked down at the diskette.

VOODOO, it said.

"...that you-do so well," he scoffed and sat down in front of the table.

Simon took another sip of coffee.

"Ah, to hell with it," he announced, and snatched up the diskette. He practically rammed it into his diskette drive and began pounding on the keys for the files to drop to his hard drive.

On his machine, he went into the VOODOO directory and executed the program.

The screen appeared just as before, with the address and the website.

This time, Simon had pen and paper on hand to write down the information.

He pushed the scrap of paper aside and opened up the file for Edgars, the school principal. A ruddy face appeared to the right of the doll, glasses perched on what would have been a red nose. *It's in black and white*, Simon thought. *So was Ellen's.*

"Yearbook," Simon said aloud. "Yearbook and a scanner."

A photo, though? All you need is a photo and you can make someone ill? How the hell would you code something like that?

Simon looked down at the paper on which he had scrawled the registration information. "Well, if I can't find out how, I can at least give you a taste of your own software, Mr. Darren Curtis."

Simon went out onto the World Wide Web and typed in the website for Houngan Software. Within moments, the home page had loaded. A snappy logo at the top pronounced that he was at the Houngan Software website, home of Voodoo!

"Yee-hah," Simon cheered with all the lackluster he could manage considering the hour.

He scanned down through the information on the page and finally found what he wanted.

"Darren's Home Page," a hypertext link proclaimed. Simon clicked on it.

Another few moments passed as Darren Curtis' home page appeared. A digitized photo sat in the upper right hand corner of the screen, a brooding young man who looked to be about twenty years old scowling out of it.

Simon wasted no time reading about the little creep's hobbies. He clicked on Darren's photo and downloaded it to a file on his hard drive. He then shut down his communications session and his browser. He was glad to see Darren's home page disappear from the screen.

Simon rubbed his hands together, ready to go to work. He switched over to the session that was running Voodoo. He clicked *File* and then *New Doll*. "Pull a little virtual voodoo crap on my sister, will you?" Simon hissed at the picture on his screen, inserting virtual pins into Darren Curtis' doll. "Be glad I'm not registered, or you'd mysteriously combust, you little shit."

Simon was inserting the fifteenth pin, this one in the doll's left armpit, when the phone rang. He had time to wonder to himself who it might be and turn instinctively to the cordless resting to the left of his monitor, before he realized it wasn't the cordless that was ringing.

It was the line he had exclusively for his computer.

The communications software, in auto answer mode, started

itself and answered the call. A small message at the bottom of the screen flashed, "Speakerphone activated."

There was a moment of silence before Simon had the presence of mind to say hello.

"Simon Carlson, please," replied the male voice from the other end.

Simon stared at the speakers. "Who is calling?" he finally managed to say.

"Oh, Simon, you know who this is, don't be stupid," the voice chastised. "This is Darren Curtis. You just accessed my website."

Simon suddenly felt as though he were trying to think through a large amount of gauze. "Darren? Darren, how did you get this number?"

"Well, you're the only user listed on carlsonsoftware.com, and that's where you just accessed my page from. I happened to be watching when you downloaded my picture. I keep an eye on who's accessing it and when. Now what exactly were you planning on doing with that picture, Simon?"

Simon was silent.

"How'd you ever get this speakerphone to work? I've got the same kind of system in the next room, and I never can get the damn thing to respond properly."

"Beta testing the new version of the software," Simon replied woodenly. "Works like a champ. How did you know what type of system I'm running, Darren?"

Darren chuckled. "Just a routine that I pass across the line when I call someone through their computer. I'm a nosy one, I am. And no, don't think I'll pass you a virus or something. That'd be very uncivilized even though, you know, your firewall is abysmal."

Simon was not sure what to say next.

"So you like my little software package, Simon? Impressed?"

"How in the hell did you do it, Darren? I looked at the files, there's nothing special about them."

Darren sighed. "Tsk tsk, Simon. Trade secret. I tell you, and then next thing you know you're coding software so people can give each other massages over the Internet. No, we can't have that." There was a pause. "Do you think I'm stupid, Simon?"

"No," Simon said, "obviously you're not to create software like this."

"Good answer," Darren's voice was thoughtful. "However, you

must think I'm somewhat less than smart to code some software that does what mine does and then not code a safety catch in it to keep people from using it on its creator." Another pause, this one with a malicious texture. "That's what you were doing, right?"

"A ten-year-old was using it to put pins in my sister's neck, you sick bastard!" Simon spat at the microphone.

"Now, why weren't you trying to get back at *him*?" Darren asked calmly. "Just remember, Simon, software doesn't kill people, people kill people."

There was silence on the line, except for the sound of Darren busily typing.

"Nice web page there, Simon," he commented. "Bad picture of you, though."

Simon went to hang up the line, but as he did a small spattering of blood hit the keys. His hand went up to his nose. When he brought his fingers back in front of his eyes again, they were crimson. "What are you doing?" he breathed at the microphone. "The code couldn't do this! The pins didn't draw blood!"

"You're good with beta code, Simon," Darren hissed. "This is Voodoo 2.0B. Not yet ready for release. Close, though, don't you think?"

Simon coughed and a large wad of blood exploded onto the screen. He fell sideways out of the chair and hit the floor, doubled over and wheezing.

"Ah, yes, sounds like it's working quite well. We'll be ready for gamma testing sooner than I thought. Thanks, Simon. Have a good rest of the evening."

The line went dead.

A half-hour later, the blood-drenched monitor turned itself off in order to conserve energy.

Of Sorcery and Seasoning

Jeff groaned as he heard something upstairs go clattering to the floor. As it became increasingly apparent that the situation was now completely out of control, he worked hard to assure himself that none of it was his fault.

It was, of course, entirely his mother's fault. She was the one who had insisted Derek's name stay on the list of invitees for Jeff's birthday slumber party. Jeff had protested as best he could at the time, but to no avail.

"All the other boys from the neighborhood are coming," had been her reasoning. "How do you think Derek would feel if he didn't get an invitation to your party? What do you think his parents will think of us?" She had smiled down at him. "And think about it another way: how would you feel if you hadn't gotten an invitation to one of Derek's parties?"

Jeff, being somewhat older and wiser now at twelve, did not consider himself to be an idiot. The games at Derek's parties normally included such droll pastimes as throwing lit firecrackers at dogs. Trying to explain this to his mother, however, would have done no good. "Child's horseplay," she would say and wave it away, although she would be unable to hide the nervousness in her voice.

Child's horseplay, Jeff thought glumly. His best friend Troy had been at the party with the firecrackers incident, watching the chaos along with all the other attending children. Derek's normal course of business was to choose a firecracker, light it, then throw it at his terrified beagle, roaring laughter as the animal became more frenzied with each detonation. At one point in the festivities, Derek had lit a rather sizable explosive ("M-500," it had proclaimed itself in large, conflagrating letters), and acted as though it would be next to send the neurotic dog into a barking fit. At the last second, he turned instead and threw it into the crowd of onlookers. "Heads up!" he yelled at the unsuspecting boys.

All of them managed to flee ground zero and dive to safety, all except Troy. Troy's instinctive reaction was to bat the firecracker away with the palm of his hand. Had he been a second or two slower, he might have lost one or more fingers. As it was, the powder burns on his hand had taken two months to completely heal.

Child's horseplay, Jeff thought again sourly.

While his father and mother slept blissfully—his slumber aided no doubt by alcohol, hers by the pills she kept on her nightstand—Jeff was dealing with the consequences of their decision to include Derek.

Part of this was Jeff reconciling himself to the fact that although his mother had most of the blame on her shoulders, he himself had knocked over the first domino.

Derek had asked what Jeff's family kept in their attic and like a moron, Jeff had told him.

The fact that at the time Jeff revealed the secret, he was being pressed face first into a wall with one arm held indelicately behind his back was not an excuse. *I could have held out, lied—something,* Jeff tried to convince himself.

"My grandfather's stuff," he had confessed to the wall, with which he had been becoming very intimately acquainted. "It's just a bunch of my grandfather's stuff."

"Can't be just that," Derek had sneered into Jeff's right ear, the larger boy's stale breath wafting around him. "If it was just that, it wouldn't have been such a big deal to tell me." Jeff's arm suddenly found that it could indeed work itself upward behind his back a fraction of an inch more.

"No, that's all," Jeff cried out. "That's it. I swear."

"Well, if that's all there is, it wouldn't hurt to just go look, now would it?" Derek suggested.

"No," Jeff panted. "We can't...we can't go up there."

"And why not?" Derek asked, incensed and kindly leaning harder against his host.

"Some of it's dangerous," Jeff blurted, knowing as he did so he was sealing his fate. But at that point, with his arm screaming at him and his head swimming with the pressure exerted against it, he had no idea what else to say.

"Dangerous?" Derek turned from his captive to leer at his fellow partygoers. They took a tentative and collective step back. "What kind of dangerous might that be, Jeffy?"

"I don't know," Jeff replied. He then gave out a small squeal as his arm was forced upward again. "No, really, Derek, I...don't... KNOW. My parents told me it was dangerous, and that I shouldn't go up there. That's all I know. I *swear*." This explanation was exhaled quickly with the hopes of gaining relief for his arm, which was steadily becoming numb.

Derek appeared thoughtful for a moment. "All right," he said finally, letting go of Jeff.

Jeff sank to the floor, cradling his arm and grateful it was over. The feeling did not last.

"But hey," Derek went on, "let's go anyway. Could be fun." He turned to the other children and grinned. No one would dare disagree with him. At five-foot-six and a hundred and seventy-five pounds, he towered over all of them.

Derek left the room with the entourage of boys following at a prudent distance. Jeff stayed on the floor where he was for a minute or two, waiting for the throbbing in his arm and shoulder to stop.

He knew he would have to get up and go after them momentarily. Derek was leading them into the attic, a place Jeff had been expressly forbidden to go.

Derek knew this, and it was exactly why he was about to commit such a transgression. Even more pleasing to Derek would be the audience he would have while doing it. Jeff might, under more normal circumstances, have shared Derek's curiosity. He was old enough to understand that a young boy's want to do something increased with each time you told him not to.

Jeff, however, had seen the look on his father's face when his father had delivered the command not to go questing about.

Shortly after his tenth year, Jeff had finally decided to ask what was behind the attic door. His mother had been getting a glass of water at the kitchen sink. His father was at the table, smoking his pipe, newspaper in hand, glass of scotch by his side.

When he posed the question, his mother let loose her grip on her glass, which splintered into the sink. His father, who had lowered his paper to look sternly at his son, took a moment to glare disapprovingly at his wife.

"Sorry," she offered meekly. She picked the pieces out of the sink, tossed them in the garbage, then vanished upstairs.

Jeff's father turned his full attention back to his son, an action that did not usually occur unless the boy had done something wrong. "Nothing is up there but a few of your grandfather's things, Jeffrey. But you are not to go up there. *Ever.* Some of them are dangerous, Jeffrey. Promise me," his father demanded, "that you will never go up there."

There was something about the look his father had given him. Something which told him, more perhaps than the words his father said, that going up into the attic was a lot more serious than cracking your knuckles or jumping on the bed. Much more.

"You gonna be all right?"

Jeff returned to the present at the sound of Troy's voice. He looked up to his friend, who offered a hand.

Jeff let Troy help him up. In the light, Jeff found he could see the scars on Troy's hand from the "accident" at Derek's party some months before. "Yeah," Jeff replied. "I'll live." He shook his head in disbelief at the entire situation. "I can't believe Mom made me invite him."

"I can," Troy answered simply. "Your dad works for his dad, right?" He looked at Jeff as if this explained everything. Jeff thought for a moment and decided it probably did.

"We should try to catch up to them before things get any crazier," Troy suggested.

Jeff did not wish to say, or perhaps could not say, exactly why the prospect of going up into the attic disturbed him so. Especially now, when the sanctity of the place had no doubt already been broken. "Some of them are dangerous," the memory of his father repeated in his mind.

At that moment, a thought struck Jeff and he slapped himself on the forehead. He almost laughed aloud with the relief of it.

"What?" Troy asked, worried. "What is it?"

"Stupid," Jeff accused himself, smiling. "The attic is locked anyway. I don't know where the key is. If Derek really wants to go up there so bad, he can wake up my dad and twist *his* arm."

"Or break the door down," Troy added.

"Well, knowing Derek he'd do both, just for the fun of it," Jeff joked.

They both laughed, the tension broken, then made their way down the hall to the other side of the house. At the bottom of the stairs which led to the attic, their smiles vanished.

The door at the top was standing wide open.

The two exchanged a quick look then sprinted up the stairs. Once there, they examined the door and found no sign it had been forced.

They then turned to look at the room around them.

Bookshelves lined every available section of wall space, filled with large leathery tomes. Huge chests, the kind pirates might use to bury treasure in, hunched on the floor and brooded. Boxes of strange trinkets shared shelf space with half-consumed candles, which bled hardened wax down their stands. An oppressively musty smell seemed to hang in the air about them, much like the dust motes which were being kicked up as Derek went about the room.

The boy was busy picking up things, remarking on how "cool" they were, then clumsily putting them back down again, usually in a place completely different from where he had acquired them. Derek's audience stood at some distance, watching silently. They were fascinated by the various memorabilia as well, but not enough to distract Derek from it. They were grateful to be granted a moment's peace.

"Derek," Jeff began, moving toward the larger boy.

"What?" Derek shot back, as he pushed a pair of spectacles onto the bridge of his nose. "So cool," he breathed to himself.

"How...how did you get in here?"

Derek looked down his nose and through the spectacles at Jeff. "Through the door, you idiot. Whatd'ya think?" Derek let out a low whoop and wrinkled up his nose. This sent the glasses crashing to the floor. The small tinkle of broken glass made Jeff wince.

"It...it was supposed to be locked," Jeff protested weakly.

"Oh well," Derek declared, marking the end of the conversation. He turned back to the onlookers. "Look at all this stuff!" He began examining a full bookshelf. Derek picked out a large volume at random and slammed it down on a nearby table, sending another cloud of particles rising into the air. "What have we here?" he seemed to inquire of the book.

Jeff took a step forward. "Derek, I don't think—"

"Oh, shut up," Derek feigned a lunge at him, and Jeff took a hop backward. "Of course you don't think. You're such a whiner, Jeffy. Don't know how to have any fun." Derek opened the book and was quite amused at the explosion of dust that followed. He began flipping through the pages.

"Wow," Derek cried out after a moment, delighted. "This is filled with spells or something! Your grandfather was into some kind of magic, Jeffy. This is so cool! And to think, I thought your family was completely lacking in coolness." He spoke this last part as though he were congratulating Jeff on some wondrous achievement.

The other children grew interested despite themselves. They began to crowd closer once it became apparent that Derek's destructive tendencies were not seeking a human target at the moment.

Jeff and Troy, however, still held back. Troy was cautioned by the painful memory of his scarred hand, Jeff by his father's voice in his ears like a mantra, "Dangerous, Jeff, dangerous..."

Jeff was about to try and appeal to whatever better judgement might be hidden inside Derek, but before he could form the words, Derek continued with his astute observations.

"Most of this is in cursive," he stated. "Jesus, Jeffy, your grandpa's handwriting sucks worse than mine!"

A slight titter ran through the young boys. Derek looked up and smiled around the room at this favorable response.

"I can read most of this one," he went on. "The part about what it does is all smeary, but what we need for it is here." Derek looked up again, mischief dancing in his eyes. "Cooool," he intoned. "Let's do this spell!"

Jeff and Troy looked at each other with shared and unspoken dread. The boy who had terrorized them every chance he could get with any and every possible thing he could use towards that end was about to start casting spells.

Derek busily scanned the page, squinting at the scrawl upon it. "Okay," he said finally. "Here's what I need. I need some rose petals. From Jeffy's mom's garden. You," he pointed at Craig, the boy standing nearest him.

Craig did not need further instruction. He was out the attic door and down the stairs in a heartbeat.

"I need some water," Derek said next. Eddie was the closest one now that Craig had been dispatched. He turned to go. "Wait," Derek called and the smaller boy stopped with a cringe frozen on his face. "Not just any water, but some rain water. It needs to have been sitting, like in a puddle, for a couple of days."

Eddie, greatly relieved, left the attic.

"Chalk," Derek read off. "A piece of chalk. There's gotta be some in all this crap somewhere."

Philip took his cue and started searching.

Derek looked down and frowned. "Mother's milk? Mother's milk?" He gazed about the room in frustration. "Where am I supposed to find some of that?"

Lee, the youngest and possibly the one who was enjoying all this the most, piped up. "We could just use some milk out of the fridge instead," he suggested.

Derek studied Lee, seriously considering this, as if he were weighing the pros and cons in his mind. "All right, good thinking. Just bring the whole bottle."

Lee smiled and then descended to find the kitchen.

Jeff finally saw his chance to cut in. "Derek, please—"

"Hang on, Jeffy," Derek dismissed him, "I'll need you in a second." He turned to Troy. "Troy, if you can believe it, the final thing I need is salt. I guess we have to make sure the spell tastes okay, or something. Be a good boy and fetch some from the kitchen, would you?"

Troy did not reply. He simply glared at Derek from across the room.

"Do it, you twerp," Derek commanded, "or powder burns will be the least of your problems."

Troy hesitated a moment more, then thought better of it. He went down the stairs and left Derek and Jeff alone in that part of the attic.

"All right, Jeffy," Derek began, "now I need you. Help me find something to mix all this up in."

Jeff was dumbfounded. He had no idea how he had gone from slumber party host to unwilling participant in whatever magical deed Derek was set on performing.

"Derek, please," Jeff pleaded. "You're going to get us all in serious trouble."

"Jeffy," Derek said in a sad voice. He moved suddenly forward, pinched Jeff's cheek and shook it. "You still don't get it, do you? Any of it, do you? Hmmm?" He grinned. "Haven't you ever wondered why I get away with all of the shit I do to you? Hmm? Haven't you ever wondered why your mom and dad could care less what I do to you?

"Your dad works for my dad. My dad signs your dad's checks. You know that? If it weren't for my dad being nice enough to hire your dad, you wouldn't have such a nice house, and you wouldn't be able to afford to go to that shitty private school you do, and you wouldn't be able to even eat." Derek let go of Jeff's cheek and then slapped him, just hard enough to sting.

"My dad *owns* your dad. And how do I know this?"

Another slap across the face.

"'Cause my dad told me so. And if my dad owns your dad, you know what that means?"

Slap.

"It means I own you, you little shit. I could kill you right here and right now, and your daddy wouldn't say boo unless my father gave his blessing. Do you understand?"

Slap. A single tear rolled of its own free will down Jeff's cheek.

"Answer me. Do you?"

As Derek brought his hand back to the ready position to deliver the next insult, Jeff realized that he did understand, all too well. Every bruise, scratch, burn—whatever Derek had inflicted upon him, his mother had tried to become furious, only to be quickly defused by his father. "Horseplay," he would say. "Kids just fooling around. Be a man," he would tell his son, "and suffer in silence."

Jeff had tried to fool himself into thinking the tone behind his father's voice was wisdom, the elder sage comforting the fledgling. Now he knew the truth: it was fear.

Fear of not getting to make partner.

Fear of making waves.

Part of Jeff's father's job as a father was to protect him, and Jeff realized that he was unable to. His father was instead held back by his own ambitions, which meant more to him obviously than the health and well-being of his son.

It was then that Jeff understood he was alone in this. Never mind that parents were supposed to keep these kinds of things from happening. Never mind that children like Derek were supposed to be kept in check by some form of authority. Never mind that a man's children were supposed to be more important than his job. Those things were in some other world, but not here and now in this attic, surrounded by the remnants of a dead relative he had never met.

This was happening. And he would have to get out of it by himself.

"Well?" Derek prompted, still ready to bring his hand across Jeff's face again.

"I understand," Jeff replied, his voice dead.

Derek nodded, apparently not comprehending the coolness with which Jeff had answered him. He brought his hand forward and caressed Jeff's reddened cheek. "Good," he smiled. "Good, then help me with this big bowl over here."

The "big bowl" in question was a cast iron cauldron, sitting under a card table and covered with cobwebs. It looked as if it could have held a small infant with plenty of room for other additives.

Jeff did not bother to push this image from his mind.

The two boys lifted it carefully. "Now," Derek explained, "over there on that table."

The table possessed a top made of slate. It was obvious from the ghosts of diagrams that it had been drawn on and erased many times. They brought it down gently for fear of cracking the surface.

Derek clapped his hands together. "Heya, Philip?" He called out. "You find any chalk out there?"

"No, not yet," Philip's voice drifted back to them. "I—wait." There was the sound of a drawer being opened and objects being shifted around. "Yeah, a whole box is in this desk."

"Bring it on," Derek instructed, smiling at his host.

Jeff's face showed no reaction at all.

Philip brought the box of chalk to the table. Derek selected a piece and began drawing the diagram from the book. It consisted of two concentric circles around the cauldron, with eight symbols evenly spaced out between them.

While Derek was finishing his work on the table, the other boys came back up the stairs and waited to be recognized.

Derek completed his task and laid the chalk down next to the book. He studied the list of ingredients. "Okay, water," he called out, like a surgeon would ask for his scalpel.

Eddie stepped forward with a two-liter soda bottle held out in front of him. It was half-full. "Here's the water," he said nervously, "but it hasn't rained in days, so there weren't any puddles, so I poured some on a rock and then put it in here. It was a puddle for all of a minute and a half."

"Fine, fine," Derek took the bottle and waved him away. Eddie went, grateful to be dismissed.

Derek uncapped the soda bottle and poured the contents into the cauldron.

"Now, let me have those rose petals."

Craig stepped up with a few spots on his hands trickling blood. He had brought three roses from Jeff's mother's pride and joy outside but not without some protest from the thorns. In another time and place, Jeff would have been appalled at the desecration of one of his mother's few pleasures. Now, he could not seem to care.

"Good job," Derek smiled and plucked the flowers clean, each red petal fluttering into the cauldron.

"Okay. Milk?"

Lee stepped up. He was holding a gallon of milk.

Derek took the container and read the label. He shrugged. "Skim. Okay, so the spell won't be very fattening."

No one laughed.

Derek emptied the entire gallon into the cauldron.

"Okay. Troy, salt?"

"They don't have any salt," Troy replied drably.

"No salt?" Derek asked, incredulous.

"None," Troy repeated. He did not seem very upset about his mission's failure. "Jeff's dad's got high blood pressure and can't eat salt."

Derek frowned and turned to Jeff. "Is he making this up?"

Jeff shook his head.

"Well, shit, we can't be stopped now," Derek fumed, "not on account of your dad's lousy high blood pressure."

Lee stepped up again. "I brought this." He handed Derek a small shaker of salt substitute.

"Hey," Derek's face brightened as he examined the prize. "This'll do in a pinch. Good job, Lee, major points." Derek slapped the smaller boy on the back hard enough to send him sprawling forward a couple of steps. Lee grinned through the entire ordeal.

"All right," Derek announced. "Let's see what we can do with this here."

"Derek, just one thing," Troy interrupted. "I mean, you haven't been taking any measurement of what the book says to use or even been using the right ingredients. If this stuff really is magical, there's no telling what it'll do."

"What, do you think we might get a demon or something?" Derek scoffed. "Well, if we do, I'll be sure to point him toward your lame ass."

The children laughed as if on cue, and Troy stepped back.

Satisfied, Derek returned to the book and studied it for a few seconds. He then unscrewed the top of the container of salt substitute and tossed the top away. He turned the container upside down and emptied it into the cauldron. As he did, he began to read from the book aloud. No one could be sure what language he was speaking in, or even if it was a language at all. No one could be sure if it was a catalog of names or commands, or if it was a chance string of consonants with vowels thrown in where they might cause the most damage to attempts at pronunciation. No one could even be sure if Derek was not making the words up, simply spouting whatever gibberish came to mind at the time.

All they could be sure of was that the words seemed to slide effortlessly out of him, and that once spoken they felt as they were hanging in the thick attic air, waiting.

When the last unrepeatable phrase was uttered, all of the boys, Derek included, waited to see what would happen. After thirty seconds of complete silence, it was obvious that nothing would.

Derek slammed his fist down on the slate table. "Well, shit. Bubble or something!" he commanded the liquid. It made no response. Derek stared into it as if expecting to find a vision among the floating petals. "Well," he said, resigned, "that's disappointing."

He stepped away from the table, hand stroking his chin as he tried to think seriously about what could have gone wrong.

Lee stepped up to him. "Derek, what if it doesn't do anything on its own? I mean, what if it's a magic potion that you use on something?"

Derek eyed the smaller boy. "Like what?" he demanded.

Lee took a step back. He apparently was not prepared for a

follow-up question. "W-well," he stammered, "I don't know exactly." The boy's eyes found a box of trinkets on one of the shelves. "But we could find out. Here." He retrieved from the box a string of what presumably were fake pearls.

The boy walked over to the cauldron, and standing on tip toe, was able to dip the string of plastic pearls into the liquid. He brought them back out again, and the entire room watched intently for something to happen to them.

Nothing did.

"Disappointing," Derek said, as if consoling Lee. "Good idea, Lee, but still no dice." He shot a glance at Jeff. "Dangerous. Sheesh."

Lee shrugged and dropped the pearls to the floor. A second later, and he shrieked. "Look! Look!"

"What? What?" came the cries of the other boys. They swarmed Lee to see where he was pointing.

Where Lee had dropped them, only half of the pearls were now visible.

"What?" Derek asked. "Where's the rest of them?"

Lee bent down and picked up the half that was still seen and pulled upward. The rest of the pearls came sliding out of the floor as if the planks were nothing more than an illusion. Lee rapped on the floor to show its solidity, like a magician performing a trick. Then, he passed his hand through the restored half of the pearls as if they too were not really there. "See? It tingles when my hand goes through it."

The boys all lined up, eager to try putting their fingers through what had been a completely solid object just moments before.

Derek stepped away from them, obviously already bored with the spectacle. He tapped a finger against the side of his face, lost in thought.

Jeff and Troy watched him closely, the only two boys not clamoring over the string of pearls. They watched Derek as the wheels turned.

He stepped over to the cauldron and began flipping through the pages of the book again.

Jeff, without thinking, moved forward quickly and rammed the other side of the table. It pitched forward and then back, causing the cauldron to spill. Derek yelled in alarm and pulled away a fraction of a second too late. He fell to the floor, then fell even further, trying to steady himself with one soaked arm, an arm that passed easily through the solid planks of the floor.

His screams of terror finally distilled into recognizable words. "What have you done?" He tried to grip his lost arm with his remaining one. He tried to get up and almost stumbled through a wet patch on the planks. He wailed, "You little bastard, what have you done? Bring back my arm!"

"Troy," Jeff hissed, "help me."

Jeff picked up one side of the cauldron and Troy, dazed, did the other. They upended it, and the discolored liquid coursed out onto the fallen figure of Derek, who held up his arms, one solid and one ethereal, in a vain attempt to prevent what happened next.

The liquid coated Derek completely, and in the moment before he passed through the floor and presumably the rest of the house and the ground beneath it, he cried out. This sound filled their ears and fell away from them as did the boy's discorporate form, echoing through the story of the house below them, then getting farther and farther away before going beyond their range of hearing.

The other boys looked like deer frozen in headlights, staring at the place where their tormentor had vanished.

Troy stood back up and looked around him, as if he had just awoken from a dream.

Jeff stepped back from the table, smiling and satisfied.

From the floor below them, they heard movement as both of Jeff's parents scrambled to respond to the cry that had brought them from sleep.

Jeff picked up the spell book from where it had fallen. He opened it and placed it again on the table.

Footsteps hastened their way up the stairs, and Jeff knew he was ready to answer any questions that might come up. Even if he did answer truthfully, which he was not certain he would do, and which he was not certain if the other witnesses *could* do, he knew those answers would not fit into the world his parents lived in.

The one which he no longer did.

He saw his father's face, flushed and confused, appear at the door.

Jeff nodded to the wet spots on the floor. "Mind your step," he told his father.

He turned a page of the book. He felt at ease.

Bottom's

Patrick crushed his cigarette out in the ashtray and proceeded to light another. This done, he exhaled a small grey cloud and stared across the desk at his guest. "So, what can I do for you exactly? Are you here to join my long list of clientele, or is there…something else."

The being in the seat across from Patrick shifted nervously, a movement Patrick considered very unlike a monarch. "I've come to you seeking my queen," he finally admitted.

"I see." Patrick stood up and moved behind his own high-backed, leather chair. "And what makes you think that I have Titania here?"

The monarch's brow furrowed. "I know you do."

"I see," Patrick repeated. He inhaled thoughtfully from his cigarette. "I've got to hand it to you, Oberon. You've mellowed out over the centuries."

Oberon blinked. "What is your meaning?"

Patrick leaned forward onto his chair, smiling. "Oh, come on now. You know exactly what my meaning is. Seems to me, not too long ago, you would have come barging in here, demanding this or ordering that. You are King of Faerie, after all."

"I *am* King of Faerie," Oberon replied. "And I did not come here to be insulted."

"Did I sound insulting?" Patrick put a shocked expression on his face. "If so, I apologize. I was merely trying to make an observation." He walked over to the private bar in the corner behind his desk. "Drink?"

"How is it that you claim to know my demeanor?" the monarch wondered aloud. "We have not met before."

"No, not as such," Patrick replied. "You could say I have merely heard…tales, is all. Still—drink?"

Oberon almost smirked. "If you know so much about me, you would know that I do not take well to earthly sustenance."

Patrick nodded, and proceeded to pour two glasses. "And if you, dear king, knew me, you would know that I cater to a very specific type of guest here at Bottom's. Therefore, I have on hand all manner of elixirs." He handed the monarch a glass, filled with a slightly bluish liquid. It seemed to glow somewhat in the light from Patrick's desk lamp. "Even for otherworldly royalty."

Oberon took the glass and studied its contents. He looked back at Patrick with uncertainty.

"Fear poison, my king?" Patrick asked. "Do not. I drink from the same bottle which I poured yours. I have no interest in harming you. Please believe me." Patrick took a long sip from his own glass.

The monarch, his mind seemingly set at ease, followed suit. "Very refreshing indeed." The surprise was evident in his voice. "But still, to the matter at hand."

"Yes," Patrick agreed, sitting down. "To the matter at hand: your queen, Titania." Patrick waited a delicious moment before continuing. "She is here."

"Very well," Oberon said, setting his glass down on the edge of the desk. "I—"

Patrick held up a finger, interrupting the king. "Would you mind?" he asked, offering the monarch a coaster. "The mahogany's real."

Oberon took the coaster and placed it between his glass and the desktop, muttering an apology.

"You were saying," Patrick prompted.

"I was saying that I wish to take my queen back to Faerie with me."

Patrick nodded and took another sip, then rubbed at the stubble on his chin. "I, myself, have no problem with that whatsoever."

Oberon raised an eyebrow, as if he had been expecting some form of resistance. "No?"

"No," Patrick repeated. "There's only one thing I don't think you've considered."

"Oh?" Oberon snorted. "And what might that be?"

Patrick gave a pause before answering. "We must consider whether or not your queen wishes to leave."

At that, as Patrick had guessed he would, the monarch stood up, almost knocking his chair over onto the plush carpeting. "Preposterous! What kind of a fool do you take me for, sir?"

"I do not take you for a fool of any kind, my king," Patrick said, smiling and remaining calm. "If you will resume your seat, I will do my best to explain."

After a few seconds' contemplation, Oberon did as he was asked.

"Do you know what kind of business I run here at Bottom's?" Patrick asked, calmly drawing on his cigarette.

"I have...an idea," the monarch replied.

"I never meant to gain such illustrious, high-name clients here at Bottom's, but it just sort of happened," Patrick continued. "I simply wanted to run the best fantasy club that I could. To give all of us mortals down here a place to go to live out our dreams. You can understand that, can you not?"

Oberon said nothing.

"No one was more surprised than I to have actual gods and goddesses among the people at the dungeon shows. And then they wanted to get involved. They wanted in on the action!" Patrick grinned. "The Lady Sif has a thing for dressing up as a Catholic schoolgirl—I mean, who knew? But if she wants to come here and do a shower scene for her own amusement, I would be a fool to say no!" Patrick leaned forward, adding in a confidential tone, "She's one of my star attractions when she works, I'd like to mention."

"What does this have to do with my queen?" Oberon asked impatiently.

Patrick's smile broadened. "Actually, quite a bit—and you shouldn't be surprised, my king, you of all people!"

Oberon tried his best to look displeased. "And what is that supposed to mean?"

"Oh, please," Patrick pleaded. "Lord Oberon, even on Earth your conquests are well known: goddesses from other pantheons, creatures of Faerie, mortal women—and men," Patrick winked at the monarch. "We've heard the stories here, my liege. We're suitably impressed."

"I—" Oberon began, but seemed uncertain how to continue. "I—"

"No, don't be modest," Patrick went on. "I realize that being a monarch for thousands of years with the same queen has the potential for being dull and uninteresting. You deserve commendation for the fact that Titania and yourself have been able to keep your own sex lives from becoming stagnant and blasé." Again, he leaned forward and spoke in a stage whisper. "The two of you seducing Hestia is a tale that is legendary, my king."

"Well, I—" The monarch was breaking into a smile despite himself. He shifted about in his seat. Patrick did not realize that the King of Faerie was capable of blushing.

"No, no," Patrick waved him off. "So humble for such a conqueror of the sheets. I understand." He stood up "Would you like to see your queen?"

Oberon stood up as well. "Yes," he said, "yes, I would."

"Very well, then."

Patrick escorted the King of Faerie through his club, taking care to use the scenic route in order to give Oberon the full treatment. He knew the old goat enjoyed everything he saw on their trip, and also that Oberon would recognize several of the scenes laid out before them. Patrick had gotten the word from reliable sources that Oberon had originated at least two of them.

The monarch had never worn studs or black leather, but Patrick knew for a fact that the Lord of Faerie had been into bondage before bondage was "cool."

Patrick drew Oberon close as they walked. Oberon had been watching the aforementioned shower scene with a degree of interest and amusement as they passed it. "It's a shame that immortal beings don't know how to let go of themselves more often," he said to the king loudly enough to be heard over the techno music booming throughout the room. "They manifest to mortals and take them, or simply seduce each other, playing games that some terrans would gladly die to be a part of, and yet they feel they have to keep an almost puritanical air about them, as if gods weren't supposed to enjoy having sex.

"Zeus," Patrick continued, "had antics that are some of the legendary best. Before he gave up his wild ways to concentrate on his golf swing, he was widely known for his bestial penchant, always turning into a bull, or a swan, or some other such thing, and forcing his furry self on some unsuspecting earth woman. Nowadays, he pretends as if his sowing of eldritch oats never occurred."

Oberon simply nodded, not speaking. The shower now out of his line of sight, he was watching intently as a naked man and woman smeared each other with what seemed to be chocolate. Though edible, as the couple was demonstrating aptly, it seemed to glow on contact with flesh. Whether this was due to something in the substance itself or to the lights in the club, one could not have been sure.

Patrick followed Oberon's gaze and stifled a laugh. The sexual revolution, Patrick thought, on earth as it is in the heavens.

Beyond the normal dungeons and demonstration rooms of the club was a large iron door. Patrick had one of the only keys. He produced it now from underneath the collar of his shirt, where it hung from a golden chain. He unlocked the door and hefted it forward, its massive weight gliding heavily but smoothly on its perfectly balanced hinges.

Oberon looked past the smaller man to the stairs. "Down there?" he asked, uncertain.

"Indeed, Lord Oberon. Indeed."

The two descended.

Beneath Bottom's was a long hallway that stretched on for about one hundred yards. On either side of the hallway were alcoves, each of which had a single door set in the wall. The only exception was halfway down on the left, where one of these alcoves had two folding chairs situated in front of the blank wall.

Patrick offered one of the seats to the monarch, which he accepted. "What are these chairs here for?" Oberon asked.

"As I stated previously, we cater to many tastes here at Bottom's. Some people like to participate," Patrick explained, stepping to the wall. "Others simply like to watch." He depressed a small panel and the blank space in front of them changed.

A large rectangular section next to the door began to slide silently upward, to reveal the viewer's side of a one-way mirror.

Oberon stood up quickly, nearly sending the metal folding chair clattering to the tiled floor.

Does he ever stand up without being overly dramatic? Patrick wondered as he reached over to steady the chair.

The reason for the monarch's distress was evident with the shield fully retracted into the ceiling. Inside the room beyond the one-way mirror was an X-shaped rack, upon which Queen Titania was bound with manacles at her ankles, wrists and neck. On the floor in front of her was a smaller dark-skinned woman, who looked to be of Egyptian origin. The Egyptian woman had her hands bound behind her back with a length of rope, and was teasing the Faerie woman with what abilities she still had at her disposal. Both women happened to be devoid of any clothing.

"I demand that you release my queen at once!" Oberon thundered.

"Whatever for?" Patrick asked simply, trying not to shudder. When the old boy did get upset, he certainly got his point across. "The Queen would be cross with me." Patrick depressed another panel on the wall.

An unnoticed speaker above them came to life, and the small alcove was filled with a sound that was quite familiar to the monarch's ears: his queen's cries and moans of extreme pleasure.

Oberon stared up at the speaker, and then back through the glass.

Careful, Patrick thought to himself, play it careful or he'll end up breaking you in half. "She'll be cross with me regardless, now that you know where she is," Patrick said.

In an instant, Oberon was upon Patrick. He pushed him up against the far wall and stared down into the man's face. Each faerie fist held a good amount of Patrick's shirt. "You have a very short amount of time in which to explain yourself, mortal," the monarch breathed.

"Please, Lord Oberon," Patrick placed his own hands over the king's. "All is well. Give me that time without your hands upon me and all will be revealed to you."

Oberon thought this over for a moment, and then complied. "Speak, then," he commanded. The king crossed his arms and waited.

Patrick adjusted his shirt and collected his thoughts. "Your queen, Lord Oberon, as you know, is a woman with a very high sexual drive. She is constantly trying to seek out new worlds of pleasure, and many of these she has visited with you." Patrick cleared his throat. "However, the two of you have, on occasion, decided that finding new levels of experience is something best done alone. Queen Titania came to me, based on my expertise and reputation, and asked me to help her find a new one."

"And what new…world would this be that you are assisting her with?" Oberon was doing his best not to snarl.

Patrick studied the monarch's face. "You would think that I would take advantage of the Queen of Faerie?"

"The thought had crossed my mind, yes."

"I assure you, Lord Oberon, that I do not derive pleasure here at my establishment. I've found that it gets in the way of my ability to run the business. You could chalk it up to the old adage about not defecating where one dines, although I find that choice of words somewhat distasteful."

Oberon nodded. "Very well. My question remains, although its meaning has changed."

Patrick smiled. "I thank you for your trust, Lord Oberon. It is well placed, I assure you." He sighed. "Basically, the queen confided to me that she had a craving for a particular kind of feeling, one that she had not been able to reach."

"And that is?"

"Helplessness," Patrick answered, and then continued before Oberon could interject. "Yes, she stated that the two of you had engaged in various games designed to make her feel completely subordinate to your whims. But the fact remained that you were there, so if she felt in danger at all, you would be able to protect her or free her or—whatever needed doing."

Oberon looked back into the room, where the Egyptian woman was continuing to attend to his wife. "And how is it you can provide this?"

Patrick stepped next to the monarch and watched the spectacle as well. He had to admit slyly to himself, it was quite the show. Eventually, he might have to move it upstairs for the paying guests. "It was all Queen Titania's idea, I must tell you. She left Faerie without saying where she was going for the express purpose of keeping you away. She wanted a feeling of helplessness that only your absence could bring." Patrick placed a familiar hand on Oberon's shoulder. "Face it, my lord. The love that you two bear for one another is the stuff of legends. I have had some of my other...clientele mention that your relationship is the standard for other immortal couplings."

Oberon looked shocked.

"I would not dream of kidding you about this, my lord," Patrick replied to the unspoken question. "Titania wished to experience what it would be like without your guiding hand and wisdom in the bedroom. To be completely at the mercy of fortune, and in this way to better appreciate you when she returns." Patrick took a moment to reflect that when it was explained like that, the whole thing almost made sense.

"You mean to say that she is doing this for both her benefit, and mine?" The king asked, fascinated.

"Yes, my liege," Patrick confided. "And pardon me for saying so, but you are a very fortunate individual to have a queen such as she."

Oberon looked into the room. The cries of his wife's happy ordeal rang in his ears. "She would not wish to see me?" he asked.

"I could certainly not prevent you from making your presence known to her," Patrick replied. "Nor would I wish to do so, if confronting her was your desire. It is my occupation here at Bottom's to provide for one's desire. However, I must warn you that going into that room would shatter that illusion she wished to create for herself."

Oberon was silent for over a minute, considering. Finally, he spoke. "It would be wrong of me to inhibit my queen's wishes, especially when she has made it clear it is for the benefit of us both."

Patrick looked up at the king. "You are decided, then?"

"I am," he responded. "I will not keep you from your business any longer, my friend. If you will be kind enough to show me the door, I will leave you to your establishment and my queen to the adventure she has devised for herself."

"My pleasure, Lord Oberon," Patrick said.

Within moments, they were at the front door of the club. None of the people coming in gave a second glance to the towering robed figure they found in their presence. "Patrick, I thank you for your time and drink. I ask that you look after my queen and make her stay conform to her wishes as best as you are able."

"It is my honor to serve the monarchy of Faerie. And please, if you ever feel that you would like to check on your queen, or perhaps—any of our other participants here, do not hesitate to call upon me."

Oberon nodded and stole a glance into the main chamber. The shower scene was winding down. "I will keep that under consideration." He smiled, then disappeared out the door and into the night. The neon of the club's sign reflected off of his cloak for several steps, blinking red and orange. Between one blink and another, the monarch was gone.

The doorman, a rather large, bald man with a Dali mustache, stepped over. "Everything go all right, boss?"

Patrick beamed. "Better than you would imagine, Arthur. I'll be downstairs if anyone needs me."

Arthur nodded and returned to his post.

Patrick stood in front of the window to Titania's room for a few moments before opening the door. The Egyptian woman on the floor did not acknowledge his presence. Good girl, Patrick thought.

"Qudshu," Patrick said softly.

The woman ceased her tireless attention to the queen. "Yes, master."

Patrick stepped over to her and knelt to untie her hands. "You may return to your room and wait for me there."

Qudshu stood and bowed to Patrick. "Very well, master. Thank you, master." In a second, her dark, naked form had vanished.

Alone in the room now, he and the Queen of Faerie eyed each other. Finally, Titania spoke. "He bought the story, didn't he?"

Patrick leaned into her, just out of reach of her bound form. "Hook, line and sinker, my queen."

She inhaled deeply. "So what happens now?"

Patrick stood back and admired the naked woman secured before him. Oh, what a weakness he had for female immortals. He shrugged. "Whatever I want."

She looked at him with the innocence of a young teenage girl, as if she were shocked by the implications. "And what do you want, Patrick?"

"Exactly what you want. You're helpless in the caring hands of a mortal, and your desire was to have this mortal do whatever he wanted to you, correct?" He reached around behind her and quietly kneaded her left buttock.

She gasped as his fingernails dug in just the right amount. "Y-yes. That's correct."

He smiled. "Then you'll understand how displeased I am that you have been addressing me this entire time as Patrick and not 'master.' You could take a lesson from Qudshu."

The queen looked mortified.

"Mortal I may be, but I do want respect," he finished.

"I—I am sorry, master. I forgot." Her face became a sly mask. "What can I do to make up for my transgression?" Her voice was low and inviting.

Patrick leaned forward so that the length of his body was pressed down on hers. The X she was bound to was tilted at just the right angle to allow for such a thing. Of course it was—he had designed it. He spoke with his lips less than an inch from hers. "I think you can stay here, trussed up as you are, alone in the dark… and think about what you've done."

With that, he removed himself from her and made his way to the door.

"No!" she cried after him. "No, master, please! Not that—I promise I'll be good, I—"

Patrick turned from where he was in the doorway. "Yes," he said. "You'll be very good."

He shut the door and turned off the lights. He kept the speaker on, though. It was good to hear the queen begging from inside the darkness of her room. How long to keep her that way? An hour? Two? Twenty-four? This would, of course, have to be considered. A prize such as she would have to be enjoyed in all ways possible.

Patrick took his pack of cigarettes from their place in his front shirt pocket. Then the shirt disappeared completely. With a furry, clawed hand he struck the lighter into life and lit his cigarette. He puffed upon it delicately, and brushed his now long hair back away from his eyes.

Puck twirled his key on its gold chain. He would finish this cigarette and then return topside. After all, running a club such as this was a full-time undertaking. "Ah," he sighed. "I love this job."

Things No One Should Know

I remember: it was a Wednesday and it was drizzling, like most days. The pavement was slick, the streets were generally in bad shape anyway, and the drivers were just as bad as they had been the day before. That particular Wednesday managed to fool me into thinking it would be like any other day. All similarities between it and any other day I had known ceased, however, when I arrived at the office.

It was seven o'clock sharp, and Donald was already at his desk. I saw no signs he had left his chair anytime during the night before. A bottle of bourbon was sitting next to his left hand and for a moment, I wanted to just turn around and go home. Up all night and working on a case was one thing, but up all night, working on a case and drinking was definitely another. Donald never did that unless things had gotten about as bad as they could possibly get. I know this from unfortunate experience. Another second later, and I was relieved to notice the ashtray was just as full as the bottle. Another fresh Camel was smoldering there on the ashtray's rim; the seal on the bourbon was unbroken.

I shut the door to Donald's office. I nodded at the bottle. "Special occasion?"

"You could say that," he replied, picking up the Camel and dragging heavily off it. Donald was quitting smoking. Donald was always quitting smoking. I believe the man had cut down to two packs a day, not that I was ever keeping score.

I did not smoke. I simply did not like the smell it left in your clothes, in your hair, in your karmic aura or whatever the hell else might be around. However, Donald was nice enough to take my feelings into account and try not to smoke around me. This sentiment did not always carry over into reality, but it was the thought that counted, so somehow that made it all right.

I looked down at the case file, the contents of which were scattered across his desk. It was the only case we were working on at the time: a personal stake for Donald. Until it was solved, we were exclusive.

Donald had had a friend during his brief stint in the army, before his dishonorable discharge. This friend had a daughter, who was sixteen, seventeen, pretty. Well built for her age. This daughter had gotten mixed up in some kind of bizarre cult, or so her father called it. To us it seemed like a harmless bunch of kids who got together to hang out and smoke some grass, but one man's circle of dope fiends is another man's wielder of pentagrams, I guess.

This daughter had disappeared six weeks before without a trace. None of her friends knew anything. None of her fellow "cultists" knew anything either. What was worse, the cops knew less than both of the other groups put together. They had marked her down as a runaway, said they'd be in touch, and shut it up tight.

That's when the friend—his name was Marcus Denny—came to see Donald.

And after four weeks of redoing everything that the police had done, we still knew only a little more than they did. And it was eating Donald alive.

Donald was never the most personable guy, but when he did manage to make a friend he did so for life. Finding Marcus Denny's daughter had become his life, and it was not working out like he wanted it to. One look at the circles under his eyes could tell you that.

"Find a bag to put this in," he instructed and pitched the bottle at me. "We're taking a little trip."

"A lead?" I asked and caught the bottle. I grabbed a paper bag from where we kept them under the coffee tray. "That would be nice."

"Not yet," he replied cryptically, dragging from the Camel

again to signal the end of the conversation. It was a trick he constantly performed and I detested. It was always easy to brush off as nothing though, for he did sign the paychecks on time. I shrugged and followed him to the garage.

Shortly thereafter, we were driving through areas of town I preferred not to enter during daylight hours, armed or otherwise. We drove by tenement buildings which had been marked for demolition and then forgotten. I could feel myself being watched, my flesh crawling as we went further into that demilitarized zone.

We passed a couple of respectable youths borrowing a hubcap from a parked Seville. "Donald?" I spoke up. "Where the hell are we going? Civilization ended ten blocks ago."

Donald let out something that seemed like a sigh. It was as if he had been waiting for me to ask the question but didn't actually want to answer it. "I don't want to do this, but there's someone we have to go see. Someone who knows."

"Someone who knows what?" I prompted.

"Someone who knows everything," he finished. To show he was finished, he pulled off his cigarette again. Here again was the sign that the game of twenty questions was over, even if I had only used up two of them.

For once, I decided to ignore the not-so-subtle hint. I needed to know more. "Okay, so you don't have a new lead for the Denny case."

"Not yet," he answered.

I nodded. "I see. But this person we're going to see knows something we can use?"

"He knows everything we can use." Donald shot a glance over at me on this. "Everything."

That's when I started to be silent and simply watch the blasted buildings drive by us. I waited for Donald to laugh and say it was all a joke. He did not. What was I thinking, anyway? Donald was never one to tell jokes.

After another two minutes, during which I had completely lost my sense of direction, Donald pulled his beatup Mustang to the front of a store. I got the idea it was a store from the hand-painted "GRO. STORE" on the front window. Other than that it looked like just another abandoned building. Heavy steel mesh covered the window, reminding me that I did not want to be there.

"We're here," Donald grunted and stepped out.

I did not immediately follow suit, so he peeked back in. He opened his coat to show me the .45 he always carried in its shoulder holster. "Don't worry," he advised. I decided to take him up on that and get out of the car.

I was immediately hit with a strange mixture of smells, of cooking chicken and gasoline. The store's front door was wide open. Donald went straight in without a look around. I lingered outside for a moment, again with the feeling that dozens of pairs of eyes were resting on me. The hair on the back of my neck stood up. I went inside.

The Asian woman behind the counter turned from the aspirin bottles she was arranging. "Oh, no," she said in broken English, "not you again." Then she began rattling off something in Chinese that must have been a string of obscenities.

"Now, Mrs. Cho—" Donald began.

"You leave him alone!" Mrs. Cho responded, switching back to English and cutting Donald off quite cleanly. "He not want you here! Took him days last time! Days! I not want see him like that again! Go!" She pointed to the door and the Mustang beyond it.

"Mrs. Cho," Donald began again, and took the bag with the bourbon from my hands. "I brought him something to help."

"Never help," she lamented. "Never stop. You," she protested, "you hurt him."

"A young woman is missing, Mrs. Cho. Now if you'll just—"

"Patricia Denny, aged seventeen," a voice called from the top of the stairs to our left. "You can let them come up, Mrs. Cho. I knew they were coming."

I wondered at this. Donald didn't call first to let anyone know we were coming, although he certainly could have done so before I arrived at the office.

Mrs. Cho had looked up at the source of the voice, but now she fixed her cold and disgusted stare upon the two of us. "Go, then," she commanded. "Do it, then."

She disappeared down an aisle.

Donald started up the stairs and I followed.

At the top of the stairs was a room, and the only occupant of that room was the owner of the voice. He was merely a shadow, however. There was a row of windows across the wall to his left, but they were covered by what appeared to be a grey blanket held up with thumbtacks.

"Can we get some light in here, Randy?" Donald asked, addressing the stranger.

Randy pulled back a corner of the blanket and let the drab daylight limp into the room. Shadows were thrown everywhere into disarray, and Randy himself was revealed.

He was a very thin young man, about twenty-four, twenty-five or so. He wore faded jeans and a T-shirt. His long sandy brown hair was tied back in a pony tail. His eyes were piercing and green and his skin was incredibly pale—pale almost to the point of being translucent.

"It's good to see you again, Mr. Stane, and you for the first time, Mr. Hartman." He directed this last part to me, and when his green eyes met mine I involuntarily shuddered. He extended his hand. Instinctively, and against my better judgement, my hand stretched out to meet his and we shook. His skin was icy cold. "You don't believe in me, Mr. Hartman. Or may I call you Daniel? Daniel, then. You don't believe I can help you, but you should, because there is much I can tell you. About many things." He smiled.

"Tell us about Patricia Denny instead," Donald instructed, not falling into such pleasantries as the handshake and not giving me a chance to think about what Randy had just said.

"No, no," Randy cooed, "not yet. Show me what you brought. I did very well. Stopped drinking three hours before you arrived. Plenty of time to bring the knowledge back. Now, you show me."

Donald reached into the paper bag, brought out the bottle of bourbon and tossed it to Randy. Randy caught it one-handed and then set it down on the floor next to his bare right foot. "Black Label," he noted. "Expensive, strong stuff." He closed his eyes. "You paid big for this. You want the information, you truly do."

It was about this time I realized the windows up there had no bars on them. Granted, we were on the second story, but still—

"We're in no danger," Randy said to me reassuringly. "Trust me." He winked at me and I felt a large lump appear in my throat.

Before I could react further, Donald coaxed Randy back to the matter at hand. "Patricia, Randy."

"Patricia Denny, aged seventeen," Randy began rattling off, his eyes never leaving Donald's face. "Mother deceased, father Marcus Denny, corporal, US Army, retired. She was born cesarean. Her mother died when she was eight. She lost her virginity to a young man named Henry Barker at the age of fourteen. Quite young indeed. She—"

"Enough," Donald said. "How did she die?"

"Oh, you're sure she's dead, are you?" Randy asked and then paused, savoring the moment before responding. "Well, you're right of course. She is dead. Died of asphyxiation. The boyfriend you spoke with lied to you, you know. She did not miss their last date, she died of a sexual joyride. They decided to try suffocation to heighten the pleasure of it. Noose around the neck just enough to…well, you know the procedure, Donald. She died with a smile on her strained face."

Donald winced slightly. It was a hard enough image for me to take, much less a guy who knew the girl in question. "Where's the body?" he asked, maintaining his composure.

"Oh, the boyfriend hid it of course. Panicked, you see. Murder, and all that, accidental or not. Dumped it in the river, weighted down with rocks, just below the Fourth Street Bridge. No witnesses to the dumping. Did a good job with the body, too. Won't come up for another month or so." Randy smiled. It was cruel. "Without help, that is." He continued. "She didn't really want to do it, you know. She didn't want a rope around her neck while he had her, but he talked her into it, and she—"

"That's enough, Randy—" Donald began.

"—tried to talk him into something else, you know, something else like a little bondage, maybe some handcuffs, to take his mind off of it—"

"That is enough," Donald repeated.

"—but in the end, you know, she really liked it. Right before she died."

Donald was on Randy in two steps. He grabbed the boy's T-shirt in both hands and spoke into his upturned face. "I said… that's enough."

"I'm sorry, of course, how thoughtless." Randy, suddenly apologetic, gave his best impression of a downcast look. "Your friend's daughter and all. Nothing more to tell."

Donald let the boy go. He nudged the bottle of bourbon onto its side with one foot. "Drink up," he said, and then made his way to the stairs.

I followed.

Randy called after us. "The boyfriend should be home around six. He doesn't get off work until five-thirty. You need his address?"

Donald made no reply. We found ourselves downstairs in the store within moments.

During the whole of the interrogation, not that Donald had asked many questions, I had felt uneasy, almost nauseous, at the string of facts that Randy had been spouting out about young Patricia Denny. How could he have known all of that? The obvious facts—parents, age, etc.—that was understandable. Other things, though...

she really liked it

...other things he should not have known. And Donald had taken it all in...

right before she died

...like it was the flat truth.

Donald read the look on my face. "Yes, all of it," he answered my unasked question. "He can and he does, the bastard."

"But how—?" I asked, looking up the darkened staircase. I knew there had to be a light socket somewhere up there, no bulb, just an empty socket connected to a purposeless light switch.

"I found out about him two years ago during another case, similar to this one, before you. We couldn't find anything. Then someone told me he was here. I didn't believe it either, but—he told me things. Told me things he shouldn't know." Donald reached for a cigarette. "Told me things no one should know." I couldn't help but notice that Donald's hand was trembling slightly as he touched the flame to the tip of the Camel.

"She sees him as a charity case. Some locals tried to kill him once, but it's hard to kill someone who knows what you're thinking and what you're going to do before you do it, even how the outcome is going to be. Needless to say, they were unsuccessful, and he's been up there ever since, drunk all the time because it keeps the knowledge out." He looked over at me. "He explained it to me just like that the first time I was here. 'I do it because it keeps the knowledge out.'"

We made our way back to the car, which was mercifully intact. There was no one in sight on the street.

We sat there in the car for a moment, saying nothing. Donald turned and looked at me. "Go, if you're going," he said.

Without being sure of exactly what I was doing, I opened the door, got out, and made my way through the store. Mrs. Cho was still nowhere to be seen. I began to ascend the wide staircase up into darkness. I reached the door and was about to knock when suddenly I felt Randy's presence there in the darkness next to me. He had been waiting for me.

I felt his breath on the side of my neck, and then I could sense his hands moments before they gently gripped my head. His mouth must have been inches from my ear, and as he whispered to me there in the darkness I could smell the bourbon in the air.

"So many things you want to know, and so little time to choose what to tell you," he sighed. "Very well, I'll just tell you the things as they pop into my head, shall I?

"Your father left you when you were six because your mother had an affair with a colleague of his. You have not seen him since, nor will you ever. He died in San Diego when you were twelve and your mother decided not to tell you. When you were eight you received that scar on your right shoulder from a barbed wire fence you snagged yourself on. When you were sixteen, you had your first sexual encounter with a woman of twenty-two which left you with a case of the crabs and the fear that you had something else. You did not. You fell in love when you were twenty-four with a woman you will never see again and whom you will never be able to replace. The woman you are presently seeing will die from something she catches in a one-night stand two years after you break off your relationship with her. You will never marry. You will work for Mr. Stane until the end of his agency, and you will live alone and die of lung cancer when you are fifty-seven. It will not be quick, but it will not be slow. You will have a fairly decent life despite, Mr. Hartman. Enjoy it."

The cold hands left my head, and he kissed me on the cheek. His presence was then gone. I descended the stairs in stunned silence.

I got back in the car. Donald had already started it up and turned it around. We were moving before I completely shut the door. We began tracing our way back through the inner city. I made a mental note to forget how to find my way back to that place.

"Give me a cigarette," I told Donald.

Donald looked at me quizzically, his lips tightly holding his own. "You don't smoke, Dan."

"I do now." He handed me a Camel. I lit it and drew in a deep double lungful of smoke. It was actually pretty wonderful.

"What did he tell you?" Donald asked after a full minute of silence.

"Just like you said," I replied. "Things..." I let it trail off. My response was clear enough.

Donald nodded. "I think we need to talk to the Port Authority about the river near the Fourth Street Bridge."

"Then we find the boyfriend," I finished for him. I pulled on the cigarette, surprised that I had not let loose with the mating cry of the smoking virgin, the cough of lungs not used to the stuff. Maybe being around all of Donald's secondhand smoke those first two years had gotten me used to it.

I would never know.

These Modern Times

The right front tire of the panel truck went down into a pothole with a sickening thump, making Al more livid than Bill could have sworn was possible. "Damn them," Al hissed, his knuckles white upon the steering wheel. "How many hundreds of years has this country been in existence, and they have yet to fix these shoddy roads?"

Bill pushed his glasses back up onto his nose for what must have been the hundredth time that evening and continued studying the roadmap. "You always have to have something to complain about," he complained. "Perhaps if you were a little more skilled at *avoiding* the holes, this would not be an issue." As an aside, he added, "Just remember, too, to keep an eye out for Lincoln Street."

Al glowered through the windshield at the road ahead and did not respond at once. There was a light drizzle, accompanied by an annoyance of fog, and visibility was reduced substantially. The wipers went back and forth, back and forth, and he hated the monotony. "Roads in Europe were never this bad," he finally grumbled, as though the conversation had not ended, but merely paused to catch its breath.

Bill let the map fall into his lap, then looked to his partner.

"Do we have to go through all of this again? We were delivering in Europe, now we have the American route. What bloody difference does it make what continent we're on? We still have jobs, don't we?"

"I'll tell you what bloody difference it makes, you old sod," Al seethed, and almost as if on cue, the left front tire dipped into a crater again. Thump, and the entire cab jerked. "There! You see, we never had these problems in Europe."

Bill looked down his nose at Al. It was the only way he could look at Al without pushing his spectacles up again. "We never had these problems in Europe, because where we were, they didn't have roads. You were too busy dodging goats and sheep to worry about potholes, you—" Something out of the corner of Bill's eye stopped him. "Oh, hells, that was it. Stop the truck."

Al applied the brakes, and the truck reluctantly slowed to a halt, skidding only slightly on the wet pavement. "What was it?"

"Lincoln Street," Bill sighed. "The one we were looking for. Three stop signs and then fifth right."

"I thought it was five stop signs and then third right." Al frowned and scratched at his cheek with a stubby finger.

"Hold on, hold on, no, it was—" Bill stopped himself and shook his head as if to clear it. "Why are we arguing about it?" he demanded to know. "How many Lincoln Streets can there be in a city with only eight thousand souls?" He lowered his voice. "Do make yourself useful, would you? Back us up a bit."

"Useful," Al grunted. "Useful, eh? Fine." He looked in his mirror and put the truck in reverse. They inched backwards.

"Yes, yes. Lincoln Street. Excellent. Go ahead and turn in."

"What number are we looking for?"

"Wait." Bill looked around the cab of the truck. "I had the form right here—" He opened the latch of the glove compartment and it fell open, spilling its contents into the floorboard: two pens; a pencil with a broken lead; a shabby romance novel that Al had been reading despite his protestations that he had never laid eyes upon it before; a wrapper to some chocolate bar long since eaten; and lastly, a substantial pile of forms, yellow, pink, and blue. These aforementioned forms scattered themselves in a perfect example of true chaos, almost as if they had a mind to do so.

"Hells," Bill repeated, with more conviction this time, studying the carnage at his feet.

"Well, go on," Al urged. "Night's not getting any younger."

"You're right, you're right," Bill agreed, and began to shuffle through the forms, looking for the one in question. "The name was Winston. Just give me a minute."

"Take your time," Al responded, pulling from his breast pocket a cigarette. He lit it and puffed upon it thoughtfully. "Remember what life was like before all of the forms?"

Bill sighed. "Yes, I do. It was paradisiacal."

Al stared at him.

"Or a necessary equivalent," Bill corrected. "Still, it was so simple back then."

"Yeah," Al exhaled a smoke ring and watched it die against the windshield. "We had an exchange to make, they told us where, we went there, we made the exchange, job done, case closed."

Bill nodded. "But Al, you understand the need for this. There has to be some semblance of order involved. After all, the population exploding like it is, we just couldn't function in the haphazard way we had before—"

Al waved off his explanations. "I know, I know, I've heard it all before. We've both heard it all before, and yeah, it makes sense when the boss explains it, but it just makes life harder on the little guys: us." He punctuated this final word by grounding the cigarette out in the truck's ashtray.

"Found it," Bill exclaimed, holding up a pink form. "Winston, twelve forty-three Lincoln Street." He attached the form to his clipboard for safekeeping.

"Twelve forty-three," Al repeated, and began driving again, scanning the mailboxes and curbsides for the number in question. "Should be on the right."

"And there it is, excellent." Bill beamed at his partner. "We might make it home before the next century after all."

Al laughed, and pulled up in front of the house in question. He shifted the truck into park, and turned the ignition off. "Well, let's get this over with."

The two climbed down out of the truck's cab and then shut their doors with practiced care toward minimizing noise. They went around to the back. Al unlocked the large door and rolled it upwards. Bill hoisted himself into the back of the truck and rummaged around in the near total darkness, studying the large packages within. He leaned out to Al, "Do you have a flashlight? My vision must get worse by the day."

Al unclipped a penlight from his belt and handed it up. "Thanks."

Within another minute, the package in question had been discovered, and Bill handed it down. He clambered down himself, groaning as he did so. "You *are* getting old," Al commented, smirking.

"Oh, shut up," Bill returned, "the only reason you do the driving is because of your back."

"Can I help it if it acts up?" Al asked, shrugging helplessly.

They shut the back of the truck, and trudged up the walk to the house.

"I remember when doing this was still fun, exchanging, you know?" Al asked, as Bill reached into his pocket and produced a small bag.

"Yes, yes," Bill muttered, only half listening as he drew out a handful of grey powder.

"It used to be a challenge, but now it's gone sour like everything else. Procedures and such. What a bother."

They made their way up the front steps and stopped on the porch.

"I concur," Bill remarked, and slowly let the powder trickle out of his hand, forming a line parallel with the bottom of the front door. He then dipped his finger in the powder, and drew a trapezoidal symbol surrounded by a circle just underneath the fisheye lens. He knocked in the center of the drawing three times. A small sifting of grey drifted away from the door.

They waited.

After a minute, Al spoke up. "Maybe they didn't hear you."

"They heard me," Bill replied softly.

Just then, they heard locks turn, and the front door opened.

A man who looked to be half-asleep appeared in the doorway. He was shirtless, his only dress being his striped pajama bottoms. "Yes?" he slurred.

"Good evening," Bill greeted the man, "you are Steven Winston?"

"Yes," Steven Winston replied.

"My name is Bill Lyle. My partner and I are here to make an exchange, if you'll be kind enough to show us your nursery."

"Oh. Oh, of course," Steven Winston said, and made room for them in the passage with a lethargic eagerness. "Please come in."

The two men made their way into the house, Bill first then Al behind him, bearing the package.

"It's down the hallway and to your right," Steven explained. "Do you require assistance?"

"No, no thank you," Bill answered, already heading down the hall.

A voice drifted out to them. "Steven?"

Steven poked his head into the master bedroom. "They'll only be a moment, Helen, they're making an exchange."

"An exchange?" Helen's voice asked, sounding as if she were still in a dream.

"Yes, dear, they're here for Morgan."

"Oh," Helen replied in much the same form as her husband had. She made as if to return to her slumber, but then stopped. "Would they like some coffee?"

Steven's eyebrows went up, and he called down the hallway. "Would either of you like some coffee?"

Al spoke up, despite himself. "Coffee—"

Bill hushed him quickly. "No thank you, sir. We won't be here long enough for that, but thank you."

Steven relayed this to his wife, who nodded assent, turned over, and went back to sleep.

In the nursery, Bill was chastising his partner in hushed tones. "You should know better than that, asking for coffee—What do you think this is?"

"I'm sorry, I forgot myself," Al defended, "but it's been so long since I had a good cup of coffee, and it's been such a long trip and all..."

"Well, never mind that. If they do too much, they'll regain awareness, and then where will we be?"

Al shuddered at this, and said nothing else in his own behalf. Instead, he fell back on ceremony, and set down the box. He ran a finger down the length of it, and the tape cut itself in two as it passed.

"Careful," Bill reminded.

Al pouted. "I didn't tell you how to draw the sigil."

"Just be careful," Bill hissed.

Al drew from the box a gossamer shapeless substance, which looked as if it were made entirely of dull cobwebs. It hung limply in his hands, only one end twitching slightly. "All right, make the exchange."

Bill looked down into the crib at Morgan. "She's such a little thing," he mused aloud, as he reached into her.

"Another 'she'?" Al inquired, standing with the grey substance at the ready.

"Yes, she. We seem to be getting just as many exchanges these days for girls as for boys. In the old days, it was a man's world only, but now women can cause just as much havoc." He drew from the little girl something as dissimilar from what Al held twitching in his hands as night from noon. It was a full bodied version of its dull counterpart, golden and positively glowing in the darkened room.

They exchanged their burdens.

"Okay, in you are, my sweet." Bill tipped his hands forward, and the stringy, grey substance dribbled out of his hands and into the little girl. The substance swam around her physical frame for a few short moments, before settling and disappearing below her surface. She shifted a little in her sleep, but nothing more.

"And in *you* are," Al commented, placing the glowing, throbbing substance into the box. He held the lid down with one hand as the other sealed it shut again. He hefted the box into his hands, feeling its increased weight. "*Whoulf*," he exhaled, "I *am* getting too old for this."

"No time for clowning," Bill explained, "let's leave before the symbol on the door gets washed away or something equally debilitating."

They walked out into the hallway to find Steven Winston leaning back against the wall, head drooped forward, snoring softly.

"Mr. Winston?" Bill snapped his fingers and the man came half-alive again.

"Hmm, what, yes?" Steven stirred, "So sorry about that."

"Not a problem, sir." Bill held out the clipboard along with a pen. "All finished, could you sign here please?" Bill had marked the blank at the bottom of the form with an "X."

Steven took the pen he was offered and wrote his signature. The ink glowed slightly for the briefest of moments, and then faded. He handed the clipboard back to Bill, who tore from underneath the top form a blue facsimile. This he wadded into a small ball and held it against the man's forehead until it sank inside Steven's skull, out of view. "The blue copy's yours to keep."

Steven shook his head as if he had been slightly startled. "Oh. Thanks."

"Sorry to have troubled you, sir," Bill said, leading Al to the door.

"No trouble at all," the man replied, seeing them out. "Be safe out there, drive careful."

"No worry of that," Bill responded with a smile as the door shut, leaving them outside alone.

The two men trudged back toward the street. "Another job well done," Al observed.

"Yes, yes," Bill rolled up the back of the truck, and was handed up the box. He inscribed a symbol, similar to the one placed on the door of the Winstons' house, on the side of the box with a black magic marker. He put it back on the shelf and climbed down.

The two men secured the back door and then climbed into the cab.

Al cranked the engine, but instead of driving on immediately, turned to look at his partner. "You're awfully quiet," he observed.

"Just thinking," Bill answered, and would say no more.

"Thinking of what?" Al urged.

"The old days, when things were simpler. Before the paperwork, and the signatures, and all. Back when it used to be interesting. A challenge."

"Yes, I know."

Bill took off his spectacles and wiped them on his sleeve. "Well, there is something to be glad of."

"And that would be?" Al asked.

"That even with all the bureaucracy in the world, there are still the ones at the bottom who can get things done!" Bill proclaimed.

"Well said," Al shifted the truck into drive; it began lumbering off. "Well said, indeed."

The truck rounded the corner of Lincoln and Third and disappeared.

Room 814

Jay Burke waited for an elevator. As he did so, he wondered aimlessly how much of his life he had spent waiting for an elevator in this exact room. Considering that on any given day, one out of four elevators—two if you were godawful lucky—was working, he supposed it could be measured in months, easily. He had been working for the Globe Coverage Insurance Corporation for fourteen years this July. He had spent all of those fourteen years with an office on this same floor of their downtown headquarters. He tapped his fingers aimlessly on the handle of his briefcase, waiting.

Forty-three seconds into the waiting, Martin Keenan came around the corner. Keenan was a slightly overweight man whose pattern baldness had formed a beachhead on top of his crown years before. Even just making his half-running shuffle to the elevators made Keenan start to breathe like a rhino in heat.

Keenan nodded to Jay, having already changed into his racquetball shorts and T-shirt. His matching fuzzy headband and wristbands made him look ludicrous, Jay had decided.

Keenan owned at least four pair—all different colors.

"You never come to the health club anymore," Keenan began.

Jay smiled, thinking, *Of course not. I don't have the wherewithal to keep up with your fashion sense, Marty. Why go and embarrass myself?* But he said simply, "It's a time issue, Martin. That's all."

Keenan shrugged. "Well, you're paying the thirty-five bucks a month," he stated, only a trace of accusation in his voice, "I just figure you'd want to put in an appearance."

Jay forced that smile to remain on his face. "Well, not this week anyway. Back on the road."

The elevator mercifully arrived. They both stepped on and the doors slid shut. After several attempts to get the Lobby button to light up, Jay succeeded.

"Ah. You're logging more and more miles every month, aren't you? They giving away a prize or something?" Keenan brayed laughter at his own joke. Jay winced a little.

The elevators, when they did actually move, were fast. Thank God for small favors. Ding, and the doors opened. Lobby sanctuary and then the parking lot ahead. "Well, I already have a toaster," Jay offered.

Keenan shuffle-ran out of the elevator, laughing some more and waving, "Make it a good one."

"You too," Jay said to him.

Jay lingered by the security desk to make certain Keenan had made his way off the premises, then he began to step forward—but stopped short again. At the counter of the security desk, right next to the sign ("Back in five" it would say for long stretches of the night) sat a plastic tray. The tray was full of all manner of keys.

A handwritten card stated: "LOST KEYS. RECOGNIZE ONE? TAKE IT."

He was mildly intrigued. Fourteen years on the road selling insurance—fourteen this July, anyway—it didn't take much. A decent movie on the hotel room pay-per-view and he was setup for the night. He rifled through the stash of keys.

Every type of key imaginable was there: car keys, luggage keys, keys to padlocks of some sort, and a single hotel room key. It was a gold-colored metal with a shit-brown plastic square at the end you held. On the square was printed, in white numerals: 814.

Jay considered it for a moment, then pocketed it. At the time, he wasn't sure why. Again, when one is driving through the Midwest selling insurance, one takes one's amusements where one can.

• • •

Thus it was that in Topeka, Jay was pulling things out of his pockets and placing them on the dresser by the television (which for the time being had the Fox News Channel on as background noise). This hotel room had the television bolted down to a device that allowed it to swivel. It also had—one of Jay's favorite Amusing Hotel Buggeries, as he called them—the remote for the television bolted down to the nightstand by the bed. It swiveled too. How thoughtful.

One night in a Peoria Days Inn, right after he had received a call from his last girlfriend that she had left him, he had spent a drunken night trying to come up with the most obtuse and wild angles to place both remote and television into but where they were still able to communicate with each other. He had fallen asleep before trying to bounce the remote's signal off of mirrors, though. For this he was grateful. He didn't like to think about that night in Peoria.

Next to his wallet and cell phone clattered down the key to Room 814.

He raised an eyebrow. He hadn't remembered still having it in his pocket. But then again, he didn't remember ever having taken it out since rescuing it from the security counter.

He picked up the key and ran his index finger over the thing's teeth. Nothing special.

Jay checked his watch. Eight-forty P.M. Nothing to do but go down to the restaurant in the lobby shortly and grab a bite. And nothing was coming on television but a couple of the *Red Shoe Diaries* flicks, both of which he had seen at least five times each.

He threw the key up in the air and caught it. *What the hell*, he asked himself.

His room was on the sixth floor. He sprinted up the stairs two flights and was pleased to note he was not panting like Keenan when he reached the eighth floor.

He found Room 814 in the hotel and walked up to it, holding out his key.

He had this terrible image of reaching the door only to have it open, a really nice looking blonde woman stepping out to go grab her own dinner down in the lobby. She would wonder why this older man was stooping forward to try a key in the lock of her room.

And, of course, so would the large muscular husband she had following her out.

Before he could complete the thought which would lead to his fantasized heavy beating, the tip of the key was against the entrance on the doorknob.

Nope. Wouldn't even go in the lock.

Ah well, worth a shot, he thought to himself.

And on it went, a minute little hobby began that he undertook on each of his stops. There weren't many contenders: only the older hotels which had not already switched to magnetic card readers or, the innovation before that: the card keys with the holes punched in them. But for those few that still used good old fashioned keys—and had an eighth floor, of course—he would meander his way up and try the key.

Jay told himself it was a silly idea, but he knew that when on the road, sometimes it was the little habits that helped keep your mind off of things. Like the fact that the girl who had left him, thus inciting the Peoria Days Inn incident—that had been his last girlfriend. And that had been five years ago. There was no one now to welcome him when he returned home.

His home, his apartment, had increasingly evolved into a way station filled with things that could do without him. His cat had died two years previous. His plants, the two he owned, were both cacti. His phone used to be forwarded straight to his cell phone, back when people would call him. Now the only people calling were clients, and occasionally the office.

At least if an angry husband were to catch him trying a Room 814's door, it would be a change of pace. But no such luck.

In the little pad of paper that he kept for important phone numbers, policy numbers, dates and the like, just underneath the cover, he put a ticky mark for each 814 that he had tried and failed to enter.

It was months down the line, at ticky mark number fifty-seven, that he found himself on the eighth floor of the Downtown Plaza, an old hotel in Des Moines that was built sometime during the twenties. The eighth floor was the top one, in fact, and back in the twenties in Des Moines, he thought, this was probably considered a skyscraper.

His quota for the quarter was in sight, but the celebratory

brandy he had allowed himself over dinner was making his head do funny things. He had a quarter-sized dollop of pain positioned right over his left temple.

And yet, the ceremony at the Downtown Plaza must be completed. Number fifty-eight must be tried.

So in front of Room 814 he stood, fished in his pocket for the key (which had never found its way to his normal keyring for some reason) and shoved it home.

Somehow, that pain in his head became a dull throb, quickly lost focus, and then vanished. He looked down in disbelief.

The key had actually gone into the lock. That had never happened before. In fact, it had only ever gone more than a quarter of the way in on one other occasion—that was when he attended that conference in Boston and wound up staying out in Everett because of a screw-up in the hotel bookings. That had been the...what was the name of that place? The Everett Regal, it had been called. Halfway in and then the key had stopped. He had heard someone moving around inside the door, perhaps in front of the mirror brushing their teeth, and had left before anything else could happen.

But now...here he was in Des Moines of all places, and on the fifty-eighth try he had found the door.

But hang on a second...that didn't make any sense at all. The key he had been given for his own room—506—looked completely different. The number for the room was inscribed on the key itself, not on a brown plastic piece that wrapped around the end. He supposed that they could change the style of their keys, but wouldn't they change the actual *keys* too?

He put his ear to the door and listened.

No sound of anything. He shrugged and turned the key, felt the lock tumble and then the door swung inward.

Standing just inside the doorway was a man with brown hair, early thirties, dressed in a brown suit. His brown tie was slightly askew, hanging just to the left, its background his white shirt. He stood there with his hands in his pockets and smiled at Jay.

"There you are," the man said. "We've been waiting on you."

Jay blinked. He tried to speak but for a moment his mouth seemed to have gone completely dry. He swallowed and tried again, "Beg pardon?"

"I said," this strange man said, still smiling, still perfectly calm, "we've been waiting on you."

Jay had the sense that there were other people in the room as well. People that he simply couldn't see, what with this greeter standing in his way. He was getting the increasing suspicion that he was exactly where he did not wish to be right now.

"I'm afraid you must be mistaken," Jay offered, wondering why he wasn't taking a step backwards right about now. "You must be thinking of someone else. Sorry to have disturbed you," he said, then pulled the door shut.

Jay stood for a moment more in front of Room 814, and then made to leave. Then he stopped again. The man inside hadn't opened the door to follow him—that was odd. If the man truly thought he had been waiting for Jay, then you would think he would try to give chase.

But it made perfect sense. Whoever else was in the room must have assured the man in the brown suit that, no, Jay Burke was not who they were expecting. Thus, embarrassed, the man had not come out of the room.

Jay decided now was a good time to leave. He looked down at the room key, still jutting out from the doorknob of the room, and gave it a brisk, but corny, salute. Then he left it there.

He took the stairs back to the fifth floor.

He made his way back to Room 506, a little miffed that any semblance of a buzz was now gone. He fished in his pocket for his room key, brought it out into the light, and then inspected it. As he remembered—it looked nothing like the 814 key that he had carried with him for so long.

Jay shook his head. Who cares? Time for sleep.

He pushed the room key home and opened the door.

He was greeted by the strange man in the brown suit.

Who was smiling.

The man then laughed a bit, "Oh no. We know exactly who you are: Jay Burke."

Jay froze in place. Had his mind been a little less out of sorts, he might have started to wonder how this individual had beaten him down three floors and gotten into his room before Jay could follow. But no, he never had a chance to ponder this, for the man *knew his name.*

"Who the hell are you?" Jay asked weakly. Over the man's left shoulder, Jay could make out one of the other people that he had been certain were in the room upstairs. This gentleman was seated in a dark, comfortable chair. Dressed in a similar suit this man was, and of similar build and age—though this man's hair was a light, light blond.

The man at the door chuckled again. Amicable to a fault. "Oh, I'm not important," he stated, "but *you* are, Jay."

Something was wrong, Jay thought. And this was a wrong that was a lot bigger than the fact this man was standing in Jay's hotel room, bigger than the fact he had brought friends, even bigger than the fact he had known Jay's name. Big enough that he could not get his brain wrapped around it just yet. But it was coming. He knew that much, at least.

"This is a joke, right?" Jay asked, knowing on some level that, no, it was not.

"No, sir. No joke." The smile was still there.

"Then...why am I important?"

The smile was gone. "You know why."

The wrongness came to Jay as his eyes flicked past the man at the door to his seated friend. *There wasn't a chair like that in my room. The walls don't look like this in my room.*

This is not my room.

Jay pulled the door shut in one thoughtless motion.

506, the room's door said.

No, you're not, Jay thought at it. *No. You're not.*

He had found the house phone by the elevators and called. It took him a moment of staring at the beige, buttonless phone before he realized what he should say.

Yes, this is Jay Burke in Room 506? I know this is going to sound crazy, but I think that somehow my room has gone somewhere else and another room has taken its place. Could you send someone please?

No. Not highly bloody likely.

"Yes, this is Jay Burke in Room 506? Well, I think I've locked my key in the room. Stupid of me, really—do you think you could send someone? Yes...thank you."

He considered waiting by his room, but not for very long. Instead he sat down on the floor by the house phone and waited. A couple of times the elevator doors opened and other guests got out, momentarily concerned about this stranger sitting cross-legged on the floor.

He gave a smile and a half-hearted wave. *No, I'm not a psychopath, thank you,* he thought at them as they made their way to their own rooms.

Eleven minutes after the call, a member of the staff stepped off an elevator. Jay stood up.

"Mr. Burke?" the younger man asked.

Jay nodded, "That's me. Sorry to have dragged you up here."

"Not at all," the man told Jay, not meaning a word of it. "Let's get you back into your room, shall we?"

Jay followed the staff member to his room and watched as he took out a pass key. He opened the door to Jay's room and took a step back.

But that's just it—it really was Jay's room.

It was Room 506.

The man in the hotel uniform was probably wondering why Jay looked so stunned about seeing the inside of his room. *Let him think I'm drunk; who cares?* Jay thought. He reached into his pocket, brought out a couple of bills and placed them in the younger man's hand. "Thanks," Jay said. "You're a lifesaver."

Before the man could respond, Jay had stepped in and shut the door beside him.

Jay could not remember sleeping but the hours passed somehow. He supposed he dozed from time to time; when he would roll over to look at the glaring red LED letters on the clock, it always seemed to be an hour or so later.

Finally, at close to five in the morning, his bladder called out to him. He sat up in bed, white t-shirt and striped dark boxers, and stood up. He stretched. His back made agreeable popping noises.

He walked over to the cramped bathroom and opened the door.

A split second later the thought entered his head, *Oh shit, I closed the—why did I—oh God, why did I close the door?*

There was his friend in the brown suit. There was Room 814.

There was that smile. The smile that made Jay come fully awake and his blood freeze in place.

"It doesn't have to be like this," the man told Jay, as though their conversation had never been interrupted from their first encounter.

"Be like what?" Jay asked, or tried to do the best he could with a mouth that was again utterly devoid of moisture. The brown suited blond man still sat in his chair, but now over the greeter's shoulder he could see a third man. Dressed the same as his compatriots, he seemed to be the youngest of the three, his distinguishing characteristic being his hair, which was the color of faded copper.

"Making us wait like this," the man at the door replied. "Making *all* of us wait. No need for that."

Jay couldn't seem to feel his knees. "I don't understand," he whispered. "What the hell do you want?"

The smile stayed on the man's face, but the mirth drained out of it.

"Oh, you know that. You know that already, Jay."

Jay shut the door to the bathroom.

He placed his forehead against the cool surface of the door. The shout built in his throat and was out of his lips before he realized it was there.

"You bastard!" He bellowed and then yelled it again. And again.

He opened the door to the bathroom and then slammed it shut. He repeated these two actions over and over again, the image of the man in the brown suit there beyond the strange strobe effect of the door. But he was, in fact, always there.

The pounding on the wall from next door finally broke through his haze. Jay stopped, the door shut; he slumped down in front of it.

"Would you cut that out for Christ's sake?" came a man's muffled yell.

"I'm sorry," Jay said to no one in particular. He crawled back towards the twin beds and pulled out his suitcase. He began to pack, throwing his belongings in haphazardly, unable to see for the tears that were welling up in his eyes. "Jesus, I'm so sorry."

Jay stopped when he reached the door to his room. Suitcase in hand, his hand touched the cool doorknob and everything froze. *Oh God*, he thought suddenly. *Oh God, what if I can't get out? What if I open the door and he's there again? What the hell do I do then?*

Rather than let this thought fester, he turned the doorknob. Click, and then the light from the hallway spilled in. He peered out and then up and down the hallway, adrenalin now clouding his system.

Maybe it's over, a voice in his head said.

You know it's not, another voice said immediately.

He looked at the bathroom door, still shut, and then walked out and shut the door to Room 506 behind him. He fought off the urge to open the door again and check. Would he find the man in the brown suit? Or his room again?

He didn't feel like tempting fate.

Skittish, he feared the elevator doors when they opened. Just an elevator car. The same fear pervaded him when he reached the ground floor, but the doors slid open to reveal the same lobby he had seen previously.

Looking like he had too much to carry, he let the bellhop open the door for him to leave the building—just in case. When he felt his heart triphammering in his chest while he unlocked the trunk to his car, he banged his fist down on the metal lid. The sound reverberated throughout the parking garage.

Open the trunk—find nothing but the paperwork and files that he kept there. Jay put the suitcase and briefcase down into their respective spaces and then slammed the trunk closed.

He stopped off just long enough to grab the largest cup of coffee he could find—catching the door into the convenience store just as someone else was leaving, how convenient—and then drove all night back to his home.

Six hours later, Jay stood at the door to his apartment. He had his keys in his hand, the key to the deadbolt outstretched, ready to do its job.

He had been standing there, barely moving, for the better part of ten minutes.

His briefcase and suitcase were sitting on either side of his feet, forgotten.

His hand simply was not up for the task. It felt like his arm ended in something made out of stone that felt alien and wrong.

Finally, he gave a long sigh and stepped forward, the keys falling to the concrete walkway with a clatter. He brought his arms up and laid them against the surface of the door. The wood felt completely neutral to his touch.

"Please," he breathed quietly, too exhausted and too terrified to care that he was addressing the front door to his apartment. "Please, just let me in. I can't...I can't deal with this. Please."

The only thing that moved now was that alien stone hand, shoving the key into the lock and turning. He kept his eyes closed and let the door to his apartment swing wide.

"You've made the right decision," the man's voice said from in front of Jay's shut eyelids.

Jay opened his eyes. Room 814 played out in front of him. The three men in their identical, thrift store brown suits were there, just as before. The only exception being the man who was sitting; he now stood at an eased kind of attention. All three watched Jay.

From this angle, as well, he could see the bed in that room. There was a body on the bed. Or at least that's what Jay's exhausted mind surmised—he could only see a pair of legs, completely bare, down near the foot of the bed. Jay could not see above the knees of that body; the wall of Room 814 obscured the rest. From here, he could not even tell what gender the legs belonged to.

"Tell me I'm dreaming," he told the brown-suited man. There was no conviction in the request, however.

"You dreamed about it for a long time, didn't you?" the man replied. "Dreamed about what you did."

Jay nodded in an almost resigned fashion.

The man smiled, a gesture that seemed poised to offer some kind of comfort. "You could be dreaming now. Or perhaps you were dreaming before and this is you, waking up. But it doesn't matter," the man said, and reached out to put a hand on Jay's shoulder. The hand did not grip Jay, it did not make to pull him into the room, it just sat there, unassuming. "It doesn't matter. We're here now, and that's all that matters. And, really...somewhere inside you you knew we'd arrive eventually. Or someone like us."

Jay nodded again. He was so tired. The bed inside the room looked so inviting.

"Come on," the man said, smiling. "You're almost home now."

Jay stepped inside, leaving his briefcase and suitcase.

The door to the hotel room shut behind him.

Grey

The key turned in the lock. Betsy heard the apartment's front door open; a series of footsteps came inside.

"Hon," Gerald called out, "I'm home."

"In the kitchen," she replied. "Your timing is perfect." She knew he would walk in, see what she was doing, then frown and do his best to be displeased. Despite all that had happened, there were a few things she still wanted to do on her own, cooking being one of them. She did not worry about his reaction. Her mind was occupied instead with the mashed potatoes, remembering that they were on the eye to her left and that the cactus helped her remember that. She squinted around for the oven mitt—she had left it sitting by the aloe plant—and then reached to where the potatoes were to remove them from the heat.

He streamed into the kitchen, a human-shaped mass of swirling color, and made the dullness all around her seem to shine. "Hi, hon," he said. As he came forward to embrace her, the deep rich green in him came forward as well, and he drew her to him with emerald arms. She felt his kiss on the top of her head.

"Hi yourself," she responded, leaning up to kiss him beneath his chin. Her imprint remained there for a moment, as though she had been wearing turquoise lipstick. It was quickly washed away by a flood of his green. She glanced down at the purplish-green hues issuing out from the object in his hand. "Gerald…another one?" Betsy shook her head, but could not bring herself to be disapproving. Her smile would not cooperate. "You shouldn't keep doing this, you know. The florist probably loves us, but you can't keep going and buying me plants all the time."

"Why not?" He set the plant down on the kitchen table, freeing up his left hand so it could stroke her cheek gently. "You need something to guide you back to the remote for the radio."

She took his hand and held it to her face. His mouth became the center of him. She recognized he was smiling, for all the colors of his body seemed to emanate from that one point. "We're not made of money, you know," she gave his hand a light, playful squeeze.

The epicenter of his colors drifted from his face to his sternum: a sign of disappointment.

"I mean—" she began, trying to correct herself or clarify her feelings or both.

She felt a finger on her lips and she shushed. "I know, I know," he began. He began tracing those lips, moving his finger along the outside of them ever so slowly. "It's just—you tell me what it's like when there's no one else around. I don't like the fact that you have to be here alone. I don't want you to be surrounded by—"

She moved his finger away. "Baby, I love purple. And God knows I wish you were here all day long, but that can't be helped. I can deal with it. I'm a big girl."

He sighed, and the colors congregated at his face again. "Big enough to make dinner, I see." As expected, he was trying to frown but his colors gave him away. They always did.

"I wanted to make you dinner. I was very careful. And I took my time, so I wouldn't make any mistakes."

No, no mistakes. She didn't need the scar on her right wrist to remind her that hot or not, an eye on a stove is grey, and just because you can't see the grey eye against a grey stovetop, it doesn't mean it can't burn you.

"All right, I trust you." He put his frown away. "I do."

They kissed again, and she could almost feel the white trickling in behind her eyes.

"Get changed, I'm almost done here." She gave him a flirtatious shove.

"Be right back," he told her, and turned. His color went with him; she heard drawers opening in the bedroom.

She put her hand out, found the counter and followed it, and the light spilling from the succulent plants, back to the stove. The grey heat was hard to miss.

"Life is funny sometimes."

That was her father's favorite saying, and he could make it fit any occasion quite easily.

She had taken it to heart, but never really understood the extent of the universe's sense of ironic humor until last summer.

Last summer was when Betsy Henderson had finally had her fill of boys. Not men, she would elucidate, but *boys*. In Betsy's humble opinion, all the males she had ever dated—from the football player in high school on whom she regrettably wasted her virginity to the overly-stable law professor terrified of commitment on any and every level—all of them had been immature boys.

Tired of the emotional strain, she had walked off the playing field, resolved never to return. All of her friends would still mention people they could "fix her up with," but the idea of it held no attraction for her anymore. "I'm taking some time off," she would thank them and say.

Not even a month passed before she discovered the two things which would drive her from then on out. One day, they presented themselves to her within roughly fifteen seconds of each other. First, the man of her dreams was standing on the other side of the cash register from her. Second, after telling him that his meal was five dollars and sixty-four cents with tax, she promptly collapsed.

That was the other defining factor, the second thing that would shape the rest of her life. To be more specific, it was tapering off the end of it.

She remembered little to nothing about the incident. She did not even remember asking Gerald for his money. One moment she was at her register in the cafeteria and the next, she was in a hospital bed. Gerald had filled in the missing time for her.

After asking for his money, Betsy's eyelids fluttered and then her eyes rolled up to the whites. She swayed, and before Gerald could react, she fell forward, her forehead connecting with the top of the cash register. A second later and she disappeared behind the counter, crumpling to the floor as though her puppeteer had suddenly called it quits and walked off the job.

Gerald told her later that no one had seemed to know how to react. He remembered everyone else standing there, seemingly frozen in time. The woman at the other register clasped a hand to her chest, her mouth forming a large O.

Gerald said he did not think about what to do, he simply did it. He dimly remembered vaulting the counter, then kneeling down beside her still body. There was a gash at her hair line from the impact with the register, and blood was coursing down the side of her face. Her pulse was weak and her breathing was shallow, but she was alive.

The preliminaries out of the way, he yelled for someone to get off their ass and call an ambulance, which they must have done for it arrived ten minutes later. Gerald never noticed, he was too busy anxiously squeezing Betsy's hand and speaking softly to her.

The first and only time they had shared their impressions of that moment, her first seizure, was in his apartment two weeks after her release from the hospital. She said he was very brave and kissed him for the first time. Gerald had blushed, smiled, and told her to thank his adrenal gland, because that had forced him into motion as much as anything else.

Then of course, he kissed her back.

It had taken some doing, but the table was halfway set before he came out of the bedroom.

"Hey, honey—" he began, already holding his hands out to offer assistance.

"Sit," she commanded and pointed to his chair at the dinner table.

Gerald moved to do as he was told. A noble green played out across his lips as he placed both his hands on the back of his chair. He was amused.

"Quit your smiling and sit," she told him. "I can still do some things for myself, you know."

His protestations began. "I never meant—" but she stopped him cold.

A finger went to her lips and he got the message. A wisp of turquoise danced from the tip of her own finger in front of her eyes. She made her way carefully around the dining room table and kissed him on the forehead. "I know you didn't. I know. I just wanted to make dinner." She shoved him down in his seat. "So get over it."

"I'm working on it," he replied; the green did not leave his face.

Good, she thought. *Good*.

When Betsy awoke in the hospital she found herself in a completely different world. Those first few moments of realization were so terrifyingly alien, she was certain they would remain vivid in her memory forever. She blinked and then blinked again, trying to change what she saw, but it did not help.

From what she could tell, she was in a bed. She could make out the vague outline of its shape, but her surety came from her prone position and the blanket she felt over her. She was in a room, she assumed in a hospital, because of the intravenous line she could feel in her arm. She was hardly able to discern it visually, and it was harder still to make out the stand next to her.

Betsy found herself lying in a grey bed with a grey blanket spread over her, in a grey hospital room. There was a grey intravenous line in her arm, held aloft by the grey stand to her left, and the reason it was so difficult for her to see was that everything, everything was grey. Grey pictures hung on grey walls, there was a grey door to her right, and the room was lit by grey light coming down from the grey overhead fluorescents. Only a dim tracing marked where one grey thing ended and the other began.

Betsy shut her eyes. *No*, she thought. *No*, she thought, fighting off panic. She began to cry, and wondered if she had gone blind. Or insane. Or some combination of both.

She opened her eyes again to see whether the world had changed back, but it had not. She felt tears rolling down her face and there in the beginnings of either panic or madness, she remembered that all hospital beds had a button or something you could push to get help. Her doctor could tell her what had happened to her, why she blacked out on the job and then wound up here and blind.

She felt beside the bed and on the wall behind her. She had her eyes shut, for she feared if she looked out into that void of grey for much longer, her mind would simply snap in two.

Because her eyes were squeezed shut, she did not see the grey door slowly open and then close again. All she heard was a voice calling down the hall, "Dr. Grant? She's awake. Please get Dr. Grant to come immediately."

She opened her eyes to look at what was coming into her room.

"You really had us worried there," it was saying, but she could not make out the movement of the lips. "How do you feel?"

It was a man—that she could tell by his voice—but his features were completely gone. Instead, she saw a swirling rainbow mass of colors that took the shape of a man. Unimaginable greens and blues swirled over his form, shifting back and forth across his frame with no apparent rhyme or reason.

No reason she could see, at least not yet; it would take time for her to learn how to read the colors.

This colorful man sat beside her bed and reached for her hand.

Her hand.

She pulled it out from beneath the covers and for the first time she noticed herself. Her hand was a dark green, with splotches of royal blue and black drifting across it. She withdrew her hand from his for a moment and brought it closer to her own face to watch her fingers cascade with hues. Her colors seemed darker and more disturbed than her visitor's. After a moment of this, she gave her hand back to him.

He took it, and she watched in amazement as a swatch of emerald green moved languidly from his hand to hers. Her forearm glowed for a moment, and then the emerald there subsided into its original darker shade.

Or was it the original shade? She would later grow attuned to the minute shifts in tone and color that danced across people's skin, but back then the difference was indistinguishable. She put her hand to his face.

The phantoms of green and blue began to collect around where his mouth should be. It was the first time she had seen Gerald smile. "God," she told him, "you are so beautiful."

• • •

Betsy hated the hours Gerald was not there, hated sitting in her hospital bed, looking around the grey dead wasteland her waking life had become.

She had tried to read a book and found nothing inside but grey letters on a grey page. To her, the book looked almost completely blank. Only after five minutes of studied squinting was she able to tell there was actually some form of writing there at all. Even the title had remained a mystery until she traced her fingers along the raised letters on the cover. She placed it aside moments later, disgusted.

The television was even more of a disappointment. If it were not for the sound, she might never know it was on. The grey of the screen brightened slightly, if such a thing was truly possible. There was nothing more.

She finally settled on a radio playing while she lay in bed and shut her eyes.

Gerald had been there to hold her hand while Dr. Grant imparted his news. She had a tumor located in her occipital lobe which was not only malignant, but growing. "The effect you are seeing, these colors, is unheard of, but not entirely unexplainable. The occipital lobe contains the part of your brain that handles visual input. Adverse conditions in that part of the brain can cause unusual impairments to one's vision."

She guessed that Gerald had already posed the question himself, because he squeezed her hand tightly when she asked. "Can it be operated on? Taken out?" She noticed how Gerald had begun radiating blue.

Dr. Grant had shifted from a balance of colors to mostly blue. This was when she had begun to learn her new language.

Blue meant many things, she decided at that moment. An overabundance of it meant sadness. *Blues musicians were right all along*, she thought suddenly. *Wonder how they knew?*

"I'm afraid not. You see, the tumor has already spread and infected your lymphatic system. Once the cancer reaches there, our options become quite limited." He took her other hand. "I'm very sorry, Ms. Henderson."

I'm sorry, too, she felt like saying but did not. She had let the tears fall unbidden from her eyes, nodding agreement. "I see," she said instead, and the irony of her words made the tears fall even faster.

• • •

The ultimate test of her control was the candle. A romantic dinner was what she wanted, and the scene could not be complete without one solitary candle. She had kept the matchbox in her pocket so she would not have to fumble around for it. Ever since the burn on her wrist, Gerald had been very protective of her around heat or open flame. Out of the corner of her eye, a spiral of purple kept moving up his body. Betsy squinted and placed the head of the match against the box. She turned to him. "Do you love me?" she asked.

"You know the answer to that," he said simply.

"Good." She struck the match and very carefully lit the candle. She shook the match out, watching the grey flame closely as she did to make certain it was dead. "Tell me what you think of the meal." She sat down opposite him. "And don't lie," she added playfully, "because I'll know."

"So you constantly tell me," he groaned comically, cutting into his portion of ham. "Yet, have you ever needed this little ability of yours for that?"

"No, it's just a little reminder."

He took a bite and then put down his fork.

"Not good, is it?" she asked, and felt her shoulders give an involuntary slump.

"Honey, it's great stuff. Glad I won't have to cook around here all the time, to be quite honest."

"Me, too," she responded. No, she did not need the ability with Gerald. She had never seen a lie on his skin. "Me, too."

Two days after her condition was made plain to her, Gerald had an idea and made a stop on his way to the hospital.

He walked into Betsy's room with the idea in his hand.

She opened her eyes and saw what she was beginning to recognize as Gerald's "signature," a certain way that his colors would act and change. It was difficult to distinguish from one person to another, more akin to knowing someone by their thumbprint, but she was learning.

"Hi," he said, and where his face should have been there was a rainbow crouching, a morass of colors in addition to his normal green.

"Hi," she replied warily. "What are you up to? And what is that you're holding?"

Whatever it was, it was like a small purple bonfire, giving off tendrils of colors which wisped away to nothingness in the air. He placed it on the counter and stepped away. "You can see it? How is it?"

She studied it for a moment. "It's purple, a deep, rich purple. What is it?"

"It's a marble queen. It's a plant. I got it on the way over."

As it continued its purplish glow, its significance to Betsy was clear: it was something that had color, and it could stay with her. She turned his attention back to him. His hues had lightened, something that she learned later signified apprehension or anticipation.

She did not even realize she was crying. "Why did you do this?"

He sat down on the bed and stroked her hair. "You need something to look at besides the inside of your eyelids."

She sat up suddenly and hugged his neck.

"Thank you, Gerald," she said. "I love it." But there was one part that she had left out, that she was *in* love with *him*. She had been working up to that feeling ever since she had awoken to find him there, but a plant was all it had taken to make it complete.

He hugged her back, and they sat there saying nothing for many minutes.

In the end, she had declined treatment. She knew from the colors she had seen on her doctors' faces she would not find respite in their therapies. It was the dark, royal blue that did it. The dark, royal blue of sadness and the shades of yellow that turned out to be lies.

Lies were interesting things to watch. Once said, they lingered on the person, staining them for several minutes afterward. Even with this awareness, she could not fault Dr. Grant and his associates. She knew they were doing it for her own good.

She left the hospital legally blind. How could you function when the world was completely grey? How could you drive a car if stop, go and caution were all the color grey? How could you keep your job if you could not read the keys on the cash register?

She accepted the disability pay and stayed at home for the longest time. Gerald would bring her flowers, all live ones, and they would sit and talk for hours on end.

When Gerald was not there, she would look out the window. The sun was a deep dark hole hanging dully in the grey sky. People would walk beneath her apartment; she would watch them to learn her new language.

There was so much black to behold. People had no idea that their green was constantly being infiltrated by black splotches which swam over their skin. She had stared in the mirror and watched the black radiate from the base of her skull outwards, and also from the nodes in her neck. She knew full well what it meant. It was a clock ticking. It was cancer.

She had less than a year to live, and she wanted to spend the rest of that time doing just that, living. Two weeks after her release from the hospital had come their first kiss, and two weeks after that they had made love for the first time. There was no time for games, no time for wondering who wanted what, it was just there. So she took it.

They made love, and for the first time since her accident she had seen white.

Years before, she had been fascinated with science. She had been a voracious student of it in high school, asking for chemistry sets and terrariums for Christmas each year. However, her passion could not write the checks necessary to get her into a university that might cultivate such dreams. Those classes and those dreams were dim memories now, but one thing swam up to the front of her mind and stayed there.

White, visible light, was the combination of all colors. When she and Gerald had made love, their bodies started out in a cataclysm of all possible shades. They switched from one to the other to the next with such rapidity that she could not follow them. Her eyes felt as if they were being held open, as their physical frames began going beyond what should have been in the normal spectrum of human vision. Colors she did not have names for danced across them, leaping from their bodies to the walls, from there sliding to the ceiling, only to drop upon them again.

And in that moment, just before their bodies could explode into each other, their colors did first. In that split second, their colors all became one, and they were the purest white. That moment of souls binding to each other, it was beyond white.

It would have made her blind to see, were she not already so.

• • •

She leaned back into his chest, listening to him read.

She had discovered something to occupy her mind while she worked in the apartment, to take the place of the books she had loved before the accident. The audiobooks Gerald brought home from the library and the bookstore helped a great deal. She was halfway through Zora Neale Hurston's *Their Eyes Were Watching God*; the tape was still in the stereo. Still, there were some books that could not be found on tape, some things that she wanted to read before she went away. "Went away," Gerald called it when he had to call it anything.

It had been Wallace Stevens the night previous. They had found a collection of Neruda's poems on compact disc, but it did not have all of her favorites. Gerald had Betsy's copy of the poet's collected verse open and read to her from the English translations.

As her thoughts trailed away, she looked down at Gerald's left leg.

A thin swatch of his green spilled over onto the grey of the couch and was quickly absorbed. She had seen this phenomenon before, making her observations from the window of the apartment.

The first time it had been a man sitting on a park bench, reading what she assumed was a newspaper, by its shape. The man was very unhappy, as was attested by the sea of navy blue that frolicked on his form. Islands of green drifted here and there, listlessly. Betsy had watched, completely fascinated, as one of these islands had gone off course and found itself on the grey newspaper.

The grey had swallowed it.

Well, she decided later, after the shock had worn off, it had not exactly *swallowed* it. "Absorbed" was perhaps a better word.

The green island stopped its movement and simply faded out of existence. One moment it was there, the next moment the grey had begun to show through it, and then the next it was gone. The hand from which the island had escaped was dimmer than it had been five seconds before.

All around me, she thought. *All around* us.

She looked down at Gerald's left leg again, to the part of the shin that had lost some of its emerald shine. She interrupted him. "We are still going, aren't we?"

He set the book down. "I start my leave of absence next Monday."

"And—"

Gerald traced a hand along her furrowed brow, anticipating the conversation. "Darling, we've been through this. I explained it to my boss, and he understands. We leave Monday." He smiled. "A cabin in the woods. Away from all of this."

She felt relieved. He resumed reciting verse to her, but fifteen minutes later she had fallen asleep with her head tucked under his chin.

She awoke later that night and could not remember Gerald bringing her to bed.

She had been dreaming in color, the real color she had known before her life had changed. Still, she thought absently, who was to say what real colors were, now that she had seen hers? Perhaps the rest of the world was seeing the outward show, while she could go past that to what was really there; to what things really looked like. She did not know and in her half-awake state, it was not a concept she could completely get her mind around.

Gerald was beside her, a slow moving network of greens and blues, all of them tranquil like the man whose body they moved upon.

She stayed awake a few moments, looking at the grey landscape that was the bedroom they shared. She should have been frightened, but was not.

Soon, she thought. *Soon.*

She watched the fern on the end table, a purple lantern, its light slowly ascending from it in waves. Eventually, her breathing evened out, and her lids began to twitch with the depth of her sleep. She and her lover moved closer together in this sleep, and their colors followed suit.

On the table, the purple spilled outward still, seeming to watch over them where they lay.

The Excavation

A plain. A plain of sand…thick, dense sand. Tan and maroon sands in a design: they make ideograms on the ground which are constantly shifting and changing. Perhaps it's spelling out something in a dead language: a prayer, a warning—who can say?

In the distance: mountains, low mesas. How far away? Hard to tell, the heat shimmer makes them dance. Perspective is easy to lose on this hardpan. The sun is an orange threat, hanging overhead.

From somewhere, a trumpeting sound of a dying animal.

There. Quadrupedal, low to the ground, they are. Naked of hair, except for just about their eyes. Evolutionary benefit: must cut the glare. Must shield the eyes from the wind kicking up the heavy sand. Such strange pink, leathery skin they possess.

The trumpet again. An awful, harrowing harrooing sound that dies away. One of the beasts has misstepped, found a weak spot—its leg is broken. Its brothers have moved back and away from it. They can smell that its time is near. Not to move in the desert is to die. The brothers, they wait. Wait and watch.

I can smell his end coming too. I can feel the sand underneath my feet. The desert floor is so hard, one has to work to dig into the grains.

Once the brother has died, they can run again. I move among them, *waiting for him to die. I trace a hand over the bumps of one beast's spine. I can feel the pores in his skin opening and closing, breathing for him. One of the pores suckles at the palm of my hand—*

—and I am back. I am back in myself, holding the fragmented bone of the beast. My own brother stands, watching me. He leans against one of the numerous large, flowering palm trees. We're in a jungle, yes, a jungle. A jungle where untold millennia ago, there was desert. And a beast that died here. Right here.

The scribe is there, and I describe the beasts to them. Their behavior. Their strange skin and large pores. The hair about the eyes. Everything that I gleaned from holding the bone.

I leave off things I could not possibly know. How they smelled. How the death throe of the one sounded. How the sun baked me—them—in their desert. I am not supposed to tunnel backwards. I am only to take away ideas, impressions. It is possible otherwise to become lost. Lost in empathy with the past. So they say, so they say.

I wish to go as far as I can without becoming lost. There is no use to being Lux if I cannot use those abilities to learn as much as possible… even if I keep the knowledge to myself.

Teryl^rex, my brother. My captain. He leans against the tree and looks at me. Did he see anything? Have I given myself away? He does not have the sight. He is not Lux. He would never understand.

He looks tired. We are all of us tired. Two cycles of downtime was on schedule and now, we are commanded to go to Gelthera^3. The orders came, the code was orange.

Orange: they are set to rehabilitate a planet and they must stop. They have found something.

I have looked over the records they sent me on the planet. A non-descript world of uniform desert. No life there as we know it. Some strange notes about the atmosphere but otherwise: perfect for rehabilitation.

What did they find? No doubt some avian creature's skull. Or the remains of a large fern. Some insignificance and yet the entire process must dead stop. Whatever remnant must be catalogued. "We have a duty to the past," so our division's motto says.

While I agree that we must study and notate these findings, sometimes I feel they should be simply tossed in a case so we can all get on with things.

The empire spreads and more worlds are needed and we serve. We go and we notate and we serve. All of us. Myself. Even Biryl^lux, my brother, who sees. He sees the past.

How nice it must be to not have to worry about the future. You are taken places and asked to see, and know, and tell.

Still, I know the captain who heads up the team there in the Geltheran project. Sumrae^rex. We were schoolmates, so many Cycles ago. Sumrae would not dead stop such a project for an avian tidbit. No, this must be something. And they wanted us specifically.

They wanted Biryl. His reports are more detailed than almost any other Lux since Dupard, and that was three generations ago.

Biryl looks tired. We are all tired. But we have orders. So we go.

I walk through the hold and look at the cases. All of the hard, metal cases.

We have not been back to a homeworld in…two dozen Cycles, I believe. I lose track of time in the present so easily.

Two dozen Cycles worth of remnants catalogued and boxed. Boxed and sealed. Sealed…and I cannot touch them.

Oh, I still carry with me what I felt and saw and smelled and tasted. I remember each and every one. Like it was yesterday.

This. This one here…this was the fibrous center of a seed pod. Yes, the box is large. The seed pod's core was roughly the size of your head. When they reached their full size, they were as large as boulders, and when they finally fell from their places of growth they would hit the ground…and explode.

No, I joke you not, they would literally explode. All the better to scatter the thousands of seeds far and wide. The rich atmosphere of that world. The sulfur. The craters where each new birth was a conflagration.

I could tell my fellows on the crew none of this. That world is swamp now. Bottomless swamp. The seed pods stopped exploding long before the Creator had seen fit to create our homeworld and call it good.

Now the core is in this metal case. Where I cannot touch it again.

This hold is full of stories like that one. Stories that everyone knows only half of. All except for me.

I've heard tell that there are worlds rehabilitated to serve as museums. There are continents filled with remnants from all across Creation. And in each display case there is the recorded speech of the Lux who impressed from it, explaining.

I imagine they let the workers there touch the remnants. They must.

Oh, to have lifetimes to spend opening cases and letting these stories out once more. Bringing them to life, if only in my own mind.

A cycle in subspace and we are there, dropping out into orbit around the planet that needs us. Gelthera sits in space, yellow and brooding. I have never liked yellow—the color of illness.

We orbit the planet twice, letting our ship run its own gamut of tests, then we descend. Sumrae has placed his ship at the site where we are needed. As we enter into the atmosphere and come out into the tan, listless sky, I can see tremendous rehabilitation units in their places, ready to be brought into service—waiting for us to give the all-clear to continue.

At the convergence of three continents we home in on Sumrae's signal. We land far from Sumrae and his camp, to protect them from the sandstorm we'll kick off as we touch down.

Biryl, myself and two of my crew take out the land rover and make our way to Sumrae, who waits at the perimeter of the finding.

"Well seen," Sumrae tells me as he takes my hand.

"Well seen," I repeat back to him. "It's been too long, my friend."

Sumrae nods. "I wish I had better environs for us than this. I have rehabilitated many worlds, but this must be the bleakest yet."

I had noticed this as I stepped out of my ship: the air smelled stale. There was enough oxygen to where we didn't need supplemental supplies, but nonetheless it was hard to breathe. Nothing stirred. There was no wind at all; the entire atmosphere felt, tasted, smelled stagnant. As though if we were not here, inhaling and exhaling, there would be no movement of anything, anywhere.

"The air is like this everywhere on the planet?" I asked him.

Sumrae nodded. "Yes. It's like the planet simply...stopped."

I nodded to one of the reclamation units. "Like your mission. What did you find?"

Sumrae smiled grimly. "It's...also unique, my friend. Come with me."

I overhear them talking outside the ship. The reclamation units had run a final scan before they settled in to begin their work. A unit had found something below the surface of the sand, and here we are.

And I should be out there. I should be visiting the site, regardless of whether or not the site is prepped for me to see.

But I cannot. I am afraid.

This world feels wrong. Lux are never far from the past, nor do they need to be holding an ancient artifact to gain impressions. When we walk, we touch the ground. When we breathe, we take tiny particles into us. It's too jumbled and non-specific to ever get a solid seeing, but it's still there in the background: life and the memory of life.

Here, outside the ship, standing ankle-deep in the sand, I feel nothing. I feel nothing when I inhale. Even less when I exhale. I slosh through the desert sands and feel nothing. It's unnerving. I feel as though I have completely lost one of my senses. The personal items I carry in my pockets—a copy of the Holy Writ, the Sacred Star—I will reach in and touch them every so often, just to get some kind of reading. Just to remind myself I am still alive and not dead like this place.

I will go when Teryl asks me to, but not before.

This world feels wrong.

When they take me to the site of the finding, I am not sure at all what to expect. Sumrae was never one for hyperbole, which is why he was perfect to be Rex.

The sweephover moves into place and begins to gently blow away the dirt with its microfans, and the artifact is revealed. But it is no artifact. Not in the sense of what we normally encounter, at least.

It is the complete remains of an animal. Ordinarily we would assume that its posture was a result of the shifting sands, of time, of anything—but this world has no time. The sands do not move, there is no wind to stir them. There is no continental shift, no sub-geologic activity. This should not be possible, that a world could lie so still, but it is there all the same.

So this creature could have potentially lain this way since its untimely death.

"I have never seen its like before," I say to Sumrae, "have you?"

"No, I have not," he responds. Then he hands me the scans the reclamation units provided. "What think you?"

As I look over the scans I see very clearly: blunt force trauma that completely caved in the skull of the creature in three different places.

"Ordinarily," I say, "I would think it could have fallen and hit its head against something. A rock of some sort. It could have done so miles from here and staggered all this way before finally succumbing. But this..."

"The creature was killed," Sumrae agrees.

"So there are other finds somewhere here." I sigh and rub at my forehead. "So we're in orange for at least another two cycles if nothing else is found."

"That's right," Sumrae tells me, almost smiling.

"Well," I say, "let's find it a lot quicker than that, so we can get on with things."

They exhume the remains from the pit the sweephover created and they lift it up intact to the surface of the desert. I have asked for a platform to hover above the sand—ostensibly to keep everything level while I work, but that is not a concern. Not really. I simply don't wish to touch the surface of this planet more than is absolutely necessary.

I think Teryl knows this, but he says nothing. I know he worries about me, but I wish he would not. I'll be well enough once we finish this mission and return to space.

They lay the remains out before me and I steel myself for what must come next. Surely there must be something to read here. It was once alive, as misshapen as it seems, so it must have something to tell me.

They have told me nothing of what they learned from the scans and I have not asked to see them. I prefer to go in fresh when I can, with no disposition to see things that aren't there. That has never been an issue with me, but still—I want to know that my reading is pure.

I kneel down in front of the bones and stretch out my hands. I place my palms against them, one on the thing's ribs and the other on a jawbone—

—and I'm back in myself again. Just as quickly. Stunned. I look around, expecting to see a different time and place, expecting to see this thing alive and hearty. But—

—something must have happened. I went in and came back out again. I look around and everyone's staring at me. Even Teryl looks concerned.

They tell me that I fell away from the remains the moment I touched them. I don't remember any of this.

I reach forward to try again and the medical officer of the other ship asks if I should pause to catch my breath.

Who wants to catch any breath at all on this desolate place? I think this but do not say it. I merely shake my head and he moves away.

I reach forward, lay hands upon it and try to focus past whatever was blocking me—
—and there are three. Three impacts. In rapid succession. A blunt object held by another like this one.
And that is all there is to see. I am back in myself again, almost as quickly, but this time without the jolt of leaving the vision.
They are all looking at me again. They're not used to me being "gone" for such a short length of time.
The murder, I tell them. And I can tell this confirms their suspicions.
The murder is all I can see. It was so traumatic that it seems to have wiped out everything else. There is nothing more. No details. Just three blows to the head and then...nothing.

Biryl has given us nothing to go on. He tried twice more once he knew how to get into whatever history these bones have, but nothing came out of it except a confirmation of what Sumrae and I suspected: this thing had been killed. Not by any predator but one of its own kind.

He wanted to go and try again to see more, but I forbad it. He looked so shaken and sickly that I sent him back to our ship. I hear he is sharing his time between his room and the chapel.

Biryl was always a sensitive soul, even for a Lux. I can understand where the idea of a murder being all there is to see from an artifact would drive one to the Creator to seek solace.

We send wideband scanners out, hovering over the surface and probing. If there were others of this creature's kind, they will find them out. The faster the better, so we can get away from this place. I will insist on cycles of rest after this. Biryl needs it more than ever now.

And this world feels wrong. Rex are not supposed to give credence to thoughts such as these, but I know I am not alone in my misgivings, though no one will give voice to them. It's like a dwelling that should be filled with ghosts, and yet there is nothing here. It's been stripped of its life and of its death and it's just...nothing now.

My relief is probably too present on my face when one cycle later we get back a large reading. Three more sets of remains of the same type as the first.

Something else troubles me...where are the rest of the remains? If there were four of them here, where was the ecosystem that supported them? What little Biryl was able to describe of these feral creatures shows them incapable of space travel—so this was their home.

But where was the rest of that home?

I hate to do so, but I signal back to the ship: bring Biryl. It's time to solve the mystery and go home.

The three other sets of remains. They are not far from the first set. Just outside the range of the preliminary sweeps they have said.

If the murderer is among them, he or she could not have gotten far.

Or she. This was no female. Little I know of these creatures, but yet I know the male bloodlust: the killer was a male, expressing his superiority the only way he knew how. With a blunt instrument.

They bring me to this second body, and at first glance, it would seem to be identical to the other. The skull appears to be intact, though, and the position of the bones is different. This body rests on its back and to one side.

Again, I reach down and touch the bones, rib and jaw, and—

—lush, green surroundings. The air is alive with the sound of buzzing, humming, animal calls. It all comes in so clearly, never before so clear. Where the ground is not obscured by large ferns, it is covered by rich soil just begging to be seeded. There is such a feeling of...potential here. It's positively crying out to me through the touch of my feet; such cries of joy at this garden of potential. Such a direct juxtaposition to the world this place has become that my head rings with the sounds that I was not there—and am still not there—to hear.

There is something else, too. Something that cuts through the animal noises and...

The murderer. He is here. He walks up through the undergrowth, and the clamor from the ground changes its tone. His head...there is something wrong with his head which I cannot quite see. It's though...his head has been bruised, but I know that's not correct. There is something, though...

Two others approach. One is holding back, the other...he is raising his voice. He's speaking in some form of...I don't know what it is, some strange guttural noises that I cannot fathom. He is...angry. He reminds me...he reminds of father somehow.

And he knows. This angry one knows what the murderer did. And the murderer...

Through my fingers I feel shame and guilt and hopelessness. But it doesn't...it doesn't matter...

The angry one grows angrier. The murderer points to the place...the place on his skull that's wrong...the mark, the sign that's there...but the angry one grabs him...

There's something sharp...some bit of sharpened stone...he pulls the murderer back by the hair...rakes the stone across the throat of the murderer...

And becomes a murderer himself.

And when he does, I feel...Something. Something stirring in the sky above me. The clouds begin to whip up and the sky itself starts to... open?

The murderer's body slumps to the lush floor as the ground begins to drink up the spilled blood. He falls into the position that they found his body in as—

—I jerk backwards out of/into myself. I find myself looking at the sky, at where the rent in the fabric of the sky should be. It's not there of course.

Teryl takes a step forward but I tell the platform to move forward to the other two bodies. I step off of the platform to the rim of the pits from which the bodies have yet to be lifted. I cannot wait. The empty sand's not-screams are almost as loud as the ground had been in my vision. I cannot wait.

I clamber down beside the second murderer. I have half a mind to look for the stone somewhere near his hand, but there's no use. I know it will not be there.

I touch the bones and—

—he's screaming at the first murderer, who has not yet been slain. Blind anger, I can feel it reaching out at me through the remains in the present, in the real world. Wherever/whenever that is/was. The victim was his son. The murderer was his son. And I can see his mind's eye...

A parade of sons killing brothers, other sons, fathers. Is he seeing the future? Is this angry creature having a vision or is it wild speculation? Some strange form of wild Lux? It matters not. He knows that that is to come. He knows that the ground, once fed, will grow more ravenous.

The sound, Creator, please the ground is so loud...

He cuts the son. Lets the son bleed. I can see his mind. And he can see the sky open.

And there is anger coming from out of the sky. Anger like...

Anger like a father as well. This is…no…

He walks back to the other creature, a female…her head is not wrong, she has no mark…but he slays her anyway. He knows there is no other way to prevent the ground and its hunger. She makes no sound as she falls. I can hear/not hear that so clearly. The lack of a cry. Almost like… acceptance.

The angry one marches a few paces into the undergrowth, to stand by a shrub. A flowering shrub of some kind that bears something on its branches. And as the father on the ground looks up at the father in the sky, he points the stone into the sky and cries out.

And I hear him. And I understand.

YOU, this creature cries. YOU, he accuses. YOU.

And the father in the sky cuts him down where he stands. The final YOU dies in his throat as he falls to the ground, in exactly the position I someday will be/could never be standing over him in. There might have been/still is a thunderclap of some kind. I could not say.

I'm too shaken by the fact that the bones are dead and I am still here. I feel myself let go of the bones somewhere/nowhere and I am still here/not here.

And the father in the sky is still there/not there as well.

And he looks down on me. The tear in the fabric of the sky that has no face or eyes and yet looks at me all the same. And I recognize Him.

And the Creator recognizes me.

YOU, he says.

And with that word, the world around me begins to turn to sand.

I have come to tell Biryl that we are almost home. I honestly do not know if he can hear me.

His furor to see whatever it was that he had to see back on the Geltheran planet—when I saw it I knew something was wrong. But I did not move fast enough.

And when he let go of the bones with his hands and not his mind, I knew all was lost. The mission. The planet. And Biryl.

I come here twice a day to feed him. He takes the food in his mouth, swallows. The Med tells me that it is all reflex and at first I did not believe. Could not believe. But Rex believe their eyes— they must—and I can no longer deny it.

His scales have turned the color of yellow and they flake off at the slightest touch. A touch which used to mean the world to him and used to sing volumes now means nothing. That is what convinces me. That I can touch him and by looking in his eyes I can see that he sees nothing at all.

Biryl is gone.

Oh my brother.

With Such Permanence As Time Has

An Indian girl lived in the brownstone. Her name was Kalpita. I had known her before, in a different time, in a different life, of which we will not speak. I will say that the last time I had seen her, she was on her way to Europe to get married to a doctor or a lawyer, or someone of some supposed prestige. How strange to see her now, back in a big American city, living in a building otherwise populated by strange demented older people, all waiting to die.

Her apartment consisted of a single room with two beds, like a hotel, with a nightstand between them and a beige telephone. There was a small table and chair set up in lieu of a practical kitchen and a dwarf fridge in the corner. In the closet, there was a hanging bag of clothes she never unpacked, three steps which led up to nothing, and walls covered in a shag rug the color of filth.

She was the only thing alive for miles.

I have no idea how the two of us, on our way to being three, ever found one another again. It makes no sense at times how people from your life who played minor roles will one day be recycled in order for you to play a minor role in theirs.

I want to say she was there because she was hiding. Hiding from her grandmother, of course—which made no sense, as the old woman was dead and had been dead for three years running. Hiding from her ex-husband, although I never found out if the divorce was ever begun, much less finalized. I never found out why she left him or why, despite her concerns, he seemed never to come looking for her.

Those were the things that drove her. She stayed inside, she sometimes sat on a lawnchair in her doorway so that she could experience a patch of sunlight descending onto her face in the afternoons, and she would smoke exactly one cigarette a day. She must have been, at the time, thirty years old. She had, I assume, simply started waiting to die early. She was always an overachiever, so I'm not sure why this surprised me. I'm even less sure of why it surprises me still.

If you're wondering why I haven't said much about myself, it's because thinking back on this, I have the same sense of myself that I do in dreams. In dreams, any details about self are unneeded—you're simply "you," whatever that means. Indeed, that portion of my life is very hazy and indistinct. I do remember that over the course of six months, the woman I had planned to marry for six years had abruptly called off our relationship and disappeared from my life. My mother disappeared from my life as well, due to cancer. My father had abandoned both of us long before I was old enough to form coherent memories about him—something for which it feels oddly necessary to thank him. Regardless, I considered myself an orphan. Although at the time I was twenty-eight, it didn't make the concept any easier to grasp. The people who brought you into this world are gone. You are, for the first time in your life, truly alone.

It was in this frame of mind that I had decided to drink. Not drink to slowly kill myself, which would be too much work—and regardless, as depressed as I was I still enjoyed breathing. I wasn't even drinking like I used to drink back in college, which involved heroic doses of anything I could lay hands upon. No, this was simply drinking to punish myself—just a little. The reason for this punishment was never fully established, nor had I sought it out to nail it down.

It was at a bar I saw Kalpita. It wasn't even a proper bar, to be truthful; it was just the closest thing I could find without expending effort. It was a bar that seemed to have had an aborted nightclub grow up around it. At one end of the bar I sat, reacquainting myself with the bottom of a glass which the bartender kept obscuring with more Black Russian. One moment I was studying the bottles reflected in the glass behind the bartender, the next I had looked to my left and seen her sitting there.

It's insane how people age. Myself, I can see the lines in my face becoming deeper, more sharply defined. The bags under my eyes that once only came out after a night poring over a research paper or a terribly solid bender...they appear to have taken up permanent residence. I've gotten to where I hardly notice them.

As for Kalpita, the process of growing older seemed to have done nothing but enhance the natural beauty she already possessed. There was something about the odd combination of features: her raven hair, her slightly peaked nose, her dark olive complexion, and eyes that seemed black beyond imagination. All of this became more refined over the ten years since I had seen her last. She was not beautiful—that was not the word I would use. I'm not a writer; I don't know the word to use. If I still painted, I could paint you the concept and perhaps then I could make you understand.

We noticed each other and then noticed that we had noticed each other. There was a shared sense of resignation: when you see someone from your past, you can always fall back on a mutual, unspoken understanding that neither of you actually saw the other. You can both pretend and thus avoid what could turn out to be an embarrassing or unnecessary reunion. But here, I believe we had drawn the same conclusion: that it made no difference whether or not we spoke and knew each other again, so there was no reason not to.

If there was any difference to her other than how she had grown older and done so effectively, it was the fact that she now never smiled. The entire time we spoke, what little we did speak, she merely sipped her drink and remained stoically without expression. She never spoke of her marriage; I never spoke of my marriage-that-never-was. For two former acquaintances seeing each other again after so long, we said nothing to each other about our respective pasts. We spoke of the present, and there was no future.

After she had half-heartedly invited me back to her place and we were walking down the sidewalk, quiet and alone together as we were, there was something else I noticed. It was not about her;

it was in my reaction to her. Years before, she had been an exotic beauty, an unattainable goal upon which I'd spent many a fruitless hour of fantasy. And though she was not diminished now...such desires for her seemed strangely absent.

It was then I was introduced to her apartment, passing shut doors behind which decrepit televisions keened into the night, seeking out ears that were beyond hearing, much less caring. We crept through the halls to her room. That summer was hot, and the bargain living quarters she had did not account for any kind of air conditioning. The room with the door shut, she explained, was stifling. So she mostly kept the door wide open all the time. After a visual examination of the room, I decided there was nothing worth stealing inside, her only property being what I have already described to you.

We sat side by side on her bed for the longest time, listening to the city rolling on without us outside her door. It would have been so easy to reach over and put my arm around her, to try and comfort her. But I had no idea what I wanted to comfort her about, or comfort myself about. I felt like I didn't have the ability to comfort, even if I had wanted to. And I had no real desire to find anything. I found myself wishing I had some alcohol there, but even that was faint and ill-defined.

It took a moment for my distracted mind to focus on what she was doing. She had placed one of her hands flat against the crotch of my jeans and my sex beneath it. She asked me if I wanted to, in the same tone she might have used to suggest any random thing that would pass the time. I merely nodded my assent, and her fingers went to work, freeing me. She bent down and used her mouth on me, an activity that had rattled through my teenage brain countless times.

I sat there and let her have her way with me, listening to the city, to the television sets down the hall, wondering at being fellated in an apartment building with the door wide open as it was. When she finished, she sat up and rested her forehead against mine for a moment only; ostensibly, to regain her balance and catch her breath. There was no tenderness to this gesture, no intimacy to feeling her against me. I took some notion of comfort in this. It was enough.

At some point thereafter—it could have been minutes, an hour, two—I made my goodbyes. She told me I could come back anytime I wanted. I told her I would.

And I did. A few nights a week I would come by her room. When she was there, we would sit together on the bed. Perhaps share some food, if either of us thought to bring any. At some point, she would offer what she had given before. Even though I never asked about it, nor did I ever really expect it, I always accepted. It was never discussed really; it just happened and then was done.

And so it went for a month or so. At some point earlier in my life, I probably would have stopped, gotten her flowers, a gift, something. Probably I would have tried to court her somehow, despite her nebulous marital status at the time. But in the state of mind I found myself in, it was not the kind of thing I could rouse myself to. Besides, even though I never shared this ghost of an inclination with Kalpita, the entire notion felt unnecessary with her, if not simply undesired.

At the end of that month is when both of us met Clare. There was a new tenant on the same floor that Kalpita stayed on—an old man who ordered sandwiches every day from the deli two blocks over on 15th. I had joined Kalpita for her early evening doorway sitting session. She had finished her cigarette for that day and was merely looking out at the city. I was to her left, on the floor, sitting with my back against the wall, my legs stretched out across the walkway.

Then Clare came around the corner. She was slightly younger than we were, about twenty-four, with blonde hair that came down to her shoulders. She had one of those button noses, the type that you never realize why they refer to someone as having a "button" nose until you see them. She was wearing a pair of faded denim overalls and a baseball cap that had the name of the deli on the front. She walked past us and stepped over my legs with a smile and an "Excuse me," then she was around another corner and gone. On her way off the floor and out of the building, she must have circumnavigated the floor the other direction back to the elevator, because we never saw her make her exit.

That was on a Monday, and the incident repeated itself, almost verbatim, every single evening of that week. Only the clothing of the three participants in this bizarre little ritual changed. On that Friday, though, is when Clare came back to us.

Kalpita had taken her lawn chair back inside, folded it up, and set it against the wall. I was sitting on one of the beds again. Neither of us knew how long it had been since one of us had spoken.

That's probably why hearing Clare's voice from the doorway had startled me so.

"Got a light?"

Kalpita and I turned and there she was. She was back in the overalls, with a different shirt underneath, and the baseball cap was off, dangling from one hand. That's when I first noticed her hair, and how marvelously strange it looked backlit by the sun setting over the tops of buildings. In her other hand she held up a cigarette. She was smiling.

Kalpita didn't say a word, but simply fished a cigarette lighter from her jeans pocket and walked in her sock feet over to the young woman. Kalpita lit her cigarette; Clare puffed from it thoughtfully and smiled. "Thanks," she said.

Although Clare introduced herself to us, she never really asked to be invited in. Kalpita had simply moved aside and let her, and Clare had come into the room and sat down on the floor. "Done for the day," she announced. "Mr. Alston was the last. Weekend arrives."

Kalpita looked completely nonplussed as she sat down in one of the chairs at the kitchen table, as though strangers walking in and beginning random conversations was perfectly normal.

"I thought I would say hello," Clare continued, "seeing as how I seem to be interrupting your evening reverie on a nightly basis."

I think I simply smiled in response. I didn't trust my voice to be able to speak, or my mind to be able to form words. This was a conversation, unfolding before my very eyes. I felt like this girl wanted something from me. From Kalpita. From both of us. At that moment, though I was smiling, I remember wanting her to leave. Quickly. There was a delicate balance at work here, and she was upsetting it.

"So you two appear to be the only people under the age of sixty for three square blocks," she said. "Did you know that? I swear, I deliver sandwiches all up and down the buildings here—you are the two youngest faces I've seen."

"Like attracts like," Kalpita said simply.

Clare smiled at that. She never seemed to stop smiling. It was attractive, and an attractive woman was simply not something that I needed at that point in my life. "So what do you do?"

Kalpita uncrossed her legs then recrossed them in the opposite direction. "Myself, I do nothing. He, however," she said, nodding to where I sat on the bed, "is a painter."

Clare puffed on her cigarette and looked at me. "Really? Painter as in, you have a name at it? Or painter as in, you do it in your garage and wish it were more than a hobby but it probably won't ever be?"

"Somewhere in between," I finally said.

"And what do you do here?" Clare asked me.

"He's helping me," Kalpita said. "Helping me do my job."

"Doing nothing?" Clare asked.

"That's right," Kalpita said. "We're taking applications. Stay awhile. Help us. It's busy work."

My fears were realized. Clare smiled, and then we were three.

My visits to Kalpita's place became more frequent, almost against my will. Sometimes it would be Kalpita and I, together alone as we had been before. But most times by the time I arrived Clare would already be there. A conversation would be in full swing, Clare doing most of the grunt work on it, Kalpita interjecting as little as possible but still enough to keep everything moving.

Clare asked questions. She had opinions. She wanted to know more so she could form better opinions. She had a vigor for life that I found, as the man remarked, appalling. Finally she demanded to see some of my work.

It's true what Kalpita said. Or was true. I was a painter, an artist. I had actually attended art school for about two years before becoming disillusioned with the entire routine and dropping out. I had kept a day job as one of those phone operators that you call to complain about your credit card balance, partly to keep myself in paint and canvas and partly, I joked, to make sure that something kept sucking away at my soul so I could be inspired to paint. I had even managed to pull some strings and get a couple of gallery showings. My paintings were beginning to sell.

I had expected this to, somehow, make me happy. And yet, it had not. It was as if there was this gap in myself, this hole, that I wished to fill. And I threw finished canvases down the void, trying to eventually smooth it over. But nothing had worked. Still, though, it was enough to drive me. The next painting, I told myself. The next one, ay, there's the rub. That would finally soothe me.

Clare persisted. Kalpita did not interject on my behalf. So a few visits later, I brought up my portfolio, a black, large rectangular case with a handle on it that looked like it had seen years of road. I unzipped it, and gave an impromptu artshow on the bed that Kalpita and I had shared with unadorned abandon. These were mostly sketches, studies, and the last was a watercolor I had done of a nude during my last week in art school. There had been something about the model's pose—something that spoke to me. I had finished three different watercolor studies of the model before I settled on this last one.

For some reason, Kalpita and Clare looked over this one with great interest. They both remarked how it was their favorite of all the others—this I could understand, for it was one of my favorites as well. I had enough information captured where I could go and create a full painting—but somehow something was lost in the translation. The moment had been captured at the moment, and could not be reignited now. I tried to explain this to the two of them. Clare seemed to understand, of course, but Kalpita was unreadable as she always was.

I thought the two of them sated as far as my art went. I thought that we could now safely return to doing absolutely nothing. Talking about nothing of interest, of consequence. The draw of such a thing was more attractive to me than anything else.

Then, one day as I was about to leave for another session at Kalpita's—perhaps trying to arrive earlier than Clare for some release of sexual tension (or not, I felt so completely detached from it all even while it was happening)—the phone rang.

There is no more alien sound in the world than a phone ringing in an empty apartment. Which is an even stranger thought when you realize, as I did, that the apartment was not empty. I still stood in it. Perhaps it was the fact that the phone no longer rang on a regular basis. In fact, I think the last time the phone had rung was with the news of my mother's passing. I stared at it for the briefest of moments, certain that I had hallucinated the occurrence.

But no, it happened again. I lifted up the receiver tentatively and said, "Hello?"

It was Clare. Obviously on a pay phone somewhere, made evident by the amount of background noise. "Bring your painting stuff."

"My—?" I remember saying, completely put out. "Painting stuff? Clare?"

She giggled at my confusion. I remember that as clear as if it were yesterday. The clearest, purest thing you had ever heard. I remember shivering despite myself. "Your paints, silly. You know. And some canvas. Whatever you need."

I stood there, holding the phone, stupefied. "Clare, what do you—?"

"Just do it," she said kindly. "Don't disappoint us." And the line went dead.

I remained as I was, holding the phone up to my ear, where the dial tone accused me of something. After a moment, I put the phone back in its cradle. Then I went about the apartment and collected my things: my palette, my paints, my easel, a series of brushes, a fresh bit of canvas. I bundled these up and set off for Kalpita's apartment.

When I arrived, Kalpita was sitting in a chair waiting for me, alone. She was dressed in a robe. "Go ahead," she said, "set up. We have a surprise for you."

I don't recall saying a word. I simply set up my easel, placed the canvas upon it, and put out my things on the one table. Kalpita watched this all wordlessly, her face closed to me. When I was ready, I grabbed my initial brush and looked at her, questioning.

"Shut the door," she said.

This gave me pause. The door to this apartment had never, in all the times I had been there, been shut. Not even when we were together on the bed—or apart on the bed, whichever it felt more like at the time—had the door been shut. To my knowledge, no one had ever ventured by and caught us in the act. But still, I obeyed. I pulled the door shut.

When I turned, Clare had stepped from the closet, also in a robe. Kalpita took her hand and led her to the bed.

Both the ladies disrobed before me and were completely naked. They moved with purpose; this had all been planned. They climbed onto the bed and posed: Clare sat down on the bed facing away from me. Kalpita sat down facing me, but behind Clare so that her torso was covered. They sat with their legs around each other so that both were resting on the bed, their bottoms perhaps mere inches from one another. They entangled together in a practiced way.

Kalpita put an arm around Clare's back and then laid her chin on Clare's shoulder and looked at me.

I am not a voyeur by practice. I don't paint nudes when I do paint nudes because I need any kind of titillation. In fact, normally I find the actual painting of nudes to be as erotic as you might find fixing some plumbing or washing your car. It's a task to be done. The fact that there is a naked person in the room while it's occurring is incidental.

But there was something in their pose—the fact that, as they were, they were both completely naked and yet entirely unexposed. No breast was showing, no buttocks, nothing. It was all skin and yet not skin at all. The contrast of Kalpita's dark skin against Clare's smooth pale skin was striking, and all lines in the pose led back to Kalpita's face and those eyes.

They were not naked. They were clothed in each other. And this affected me on some level that I still cannot explain.

I took a moment, and without thinking, I began to paint. I'm not sure how long I took to get the initial pose down, but I worked quickly. When a vision like this is before an artist, whether it's two women posing or a tree in the right light...you take no chances. You capture it, as fast and as efficiently as possible.

I remember my hand being steady, as if it were a tool and not the thing actually holding the tool. I remember looking at the two of them with such distance, as I normally beheld my subjects, but yet—there was an intimacy in that room that I cannot describe.

I don't know how they held that pose for so long. Later I would find it was two hours—two hours to produce what I did—but still, it felt like days.

I did Kalpita's eyes last. Two immensely clear dots of brownish black, staring at the viewer—staring at me—from over an ocean of pale flesh.

I put my brush aside and I sat down.

I remember someone saying—I think it was Kalpita, "He's done," and I heard them untangle. I heard them rise from the bed, I heard vertebrae snap gleefully, I heard them make satisfied stretching noises. Then they both walked over, still naked, to view what I had made of them.

They appraised it and both seemed satisfied. "What will you call it?" Clare asked.

"*The Two Graces*," Kalpita answered for me.

"And you are...splendor and abundance?" I asked.

Kalpita nodded. "You won't be needing the third one," she said. Then she took my face gently in her hands. And she kissed me on the mouth. The only time in our whole relationship that she did so.

Then Clare did the same. Kissed me on the mouth.

These were...odd kisses. Not passionate, though not completely lacking in passion. I have no way to describe them. They didn't feel like a reward. I felt as though I already had the reward.

The rest of the evening passed without incident. They both had gotten fully dressed and acted as though nothing had happened. The conversation was mostly between the two of them, for I was rapt in staring at the picture I had created.

It was the best thing I had ever painted. I knew it the moment I had put brush to canvas. It was also the last thing I ever painted.

Eventually, I made my way home, carrying my work with me. When I arrived, I hung it in the foyer. It's stayed there ever since.

This is the part where you, my reader—if there is indeed ever a reader for this—will wonder about the ending, though, in reality, I've already given it to you. Everything ended with that one painting.

Oh, certainly, a couple of weeks later, I went to Kalpita's to find the door shut again—but this time, forever. She had moved away and left no forwarding address. Perhaps her husband had found her, her family, or perhaps she just didn't want me to find her. I don't know, and perhaps I never will.

Clare and I stayed in touch for a while. I think we might have gone out on what passed for dates a couple of times, but eventually I lost interest. There was just something missing in her that I always saw in her with Kalpita present. There was something about the two of them together, something I had captured in that painting—and now, it was gone. It was one of those odd, once in a lifetime moments—and I couldn't get back to it, no matter how hard I tried.

As I said, I stopped painting. There didn't seem to be much point, as I had somehow sapped myself of everything I had wanted to say—everything I wanted—in that one picture which hung in my foyer. Every so often I try to pick up a brush again, but there just doesn't seem to be any point. The lines mean nothing to me now.

When someone does make it by the apartment, they stand and stare at *The Two Graces* in my foyer. If I had told you the offers I had turned down to sell it, you would be amazed. Or perhaps not.

I see it myself every day on my way to my cubicle. And I see it every night upon my return. Kalpita's eyes call to me from the canvas, inviting me to...what? I do not know.

As I stand in the fading light from the windows, with all dark in my apartment, with nothing visible but the places on Clare's back uncovered by Indian skin—and two brown pinpoints of eyes—I can't help but wonder why she did it. Why both of them did it, together. Why they gave me this gift that I can't seem to shake, no matter how hard I try to pretend that I'm trying.

If you had known beforehand that a single moment could rule you so completely, would you have allowed the moment to transpire? In the end, was it worth it?

At odd hours of the night and morning, I wonder why she condemned me to such an existence. Why I have condemned myself is a question I have not yet begun to contemplate.

Gratitude:

To my wife, Maegan, for her support during the arduous process of putting this together. And as well to Jenna Leith, to whom this book is dedicated.

Thanks as well to the editors who chose to take chances on stories now collected here. And to the others who did not.

Numerous artists also assisted in the shaping of these stories. The late Thomas Fuller did so directly; the late poet Dwight Humphries did so indirectly. They are both missed. Much of what is in this book could not have been possible without Ray Bradbury and his *Zen in the Art of Writing*. Henry Rollins deserves thanks for providing an excellent example to follow.

Appreciation must be given to my parents and other family members, as well as the countless people who have been assaulted by these stories in their various forms over the years.

John Robinson
Atlanta
August 2004